Fake to the right.
Dribble behind your back.
Move to the left.
Rocket into the air.
Jump. Shoot.
You're in!

You've made your basket, Henry. Now, do it again and again and again. It takes practice to be a basketball star. You're only twelve, but you're good at it already. Someday, Henry, you'll be a high school star. The colleges will beg to have you. You'll rack up points for your team year after year—and, finally, you'll make it to the pros.

Do it again, Henry. Jump! Shoot! Please your dad and your mom. Play the game. Basketball. Your game, your life . . .

ONE ON ONE

A novel by
Jerry Segal

Based on the screenplay by
Robby Benson &
Jerry Segal

WARNER BOOKS

A Warner Communications Company

WARNER BOOKS EDITION

ISBN 0-446-89661-6

Warner Books, Inc., 75 Rockefeller Plaza, New York, N.Y. 10019

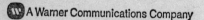 A Warner Communications Company

Printed in the United States of America

Not associated with Warner Press, Inc. of Anderson, Indiana

First Printing: August, 1977

20 19 18 17 16 15 14

For Ann . . .

ONE
ON
ONE

BOOK ONE

I

When Uncle Sam drafted him in 1949, Jerome Steele was a twenty-two-year-old country boy, as green as summer apples. The farthest he had ever been from his parents' farm was an annual fifty-mile pilgrimage to the nearest town, Nacogdoches, Texas. There, on the first Saturday of each September, his daddy unfailingly bought Jerome school clothes for the year—two blue Chambray shirts, two pairs of khaki pants, one pair of high-top work shoes—as well as several ducking cotton sacks, which Jerome, his brothers and sisters and his parents would use that fall when the family Steele went to its knees to pick cotton from their meager acres.

A child during the great depression, Jerome gained his formal education in a one-room school. His fellow pupils ranged in age from six to twenty. The school did not meet during the autumn harvesting or the spring planting. As the Bible says: Without bread there is no knowledge. The scriptures were much quoted in Jerome's county.

The year the Enola Gay atomized Hiroshima, Jerome received his high-school diploma and registered for the draft. However, Hitler and Tojo had just fallen, and Mussolini hung upside down from a tree in ignominious death. America did not need Jerome. So between 1945 and 1949 he worked shoulder to shoulder with his daddy, plowing, planting and picking. So far as was known, not one high-school graduate from Jerome's sparsely populated school district had ever gone on to

11

college. Thus, quite naturally, Jerome nurtured no ambition or life plan beyond following in his daddy's loamy footsteps. But in 1949 came Harry Truman's greetings. Jerome's commander-in-chief ordered him to Dallas for induction into the army.

Jerome had never been to a big city. The uprooted boy who got off the bus at the Dixie Trailways station in Dallas was filled with ignorance and fear.

His first fifteen minutes in the army reversed the course of Jerome's young life.

The sergeant in charge of the inductees was an evil crag of a man, meaner than dry August. His swinish eyes measured the new recruits sitting bewildered on benches before him, and his malignant leer made it quickly obvious that the veteran soldier despised the better-dressed city boys and bespectacled college men. When his gaze had completely raked the entire group, the sergeant's eyes came back to Jerome, the seediest of all the hayseeds in the assemblage. A grin deepened the malevolence on the old-timer's face. Jerome was exactly the man the sergeant sought.

"You!" he thundered at Jerome.

Poor Jerome could barely breathe. Adrenalin exploded through his body, constricted his gut, raced his heart.

"Yeah, you! Stand up!" the topkick roared at Jerome.

Jerome stood on shaking legs. But none of his fellow recruits noticed his trembling. In years past, Jerome had handled many recalcitrant plow horses. If such a plow horse knows his handler is frightened of him, the beast will kick or bite, depending on which end of the horse its victim is nearest. Consequently, Jerome learned early on, the hard way, not to show fear. So now, though terrified, he looked at the topkick with apparent equanimity.

The sergeant sneered at all the city and college types in the room, then said to Jerome, "All right, country.

12

You're the squad leader of this bunch of marshmallow asses."

Jerome forced himself to focus on the sergeant's face, fought to keep from fainting dead away.

"What's your name, country!"

Remembering the plow horses, Jerome screamed right back, "Jerome Steele!"

The topkick seemed pleased that Jerome screamed back. "Steele," the old soldier bellowed, "me and you is gonna wean this bunch of sissies from their mommies' sugar tits! Right?"

"Right," Jerome bellowed back.

"Whenever *I* tell *you* somethin', *you* tell *them!* Right?"

"Right!"

The sergeant charged to the street door of the induction center and stepped a step outside.

"Get 'em up on their feet, Steele," the sergeant roared from the sidewalk.

The next five seconds changed the course of Jerome's life.

"Get up on your feet," he yelled.

Miracle! Jerome knew how Joshua felt at Jericho, how Moses felt on Mount Sinai. No sooner had the words reverberated from Jerome's mouth than—*they all got up on their feet!*

"Tell 'em to pick up their gear," the topkick shouted.

"Pick up your gear," Jerome shouted.

Instantly, the draftees all picked up their gear. The fury of Jerome's heartbeat abated. His breathing became more normal. The hot fear began to mellow into a glow.

"Line 'em up single file 'gainst the wall," roared the sergeant.

"Line up single file 'gainst the wall," roared Jerome. One bespectacled recruit was slow in following Jerome's order. "Line up 'gainst the cotton-pickin' wall, I said!" Jerome roared again. The tardy recruit jumped a little,

13

then lined up with alacrity. Jerome suppressed a smile.

"Tell 'em to come this way," the topkick thundered.

"Go that way," Jerome shouted, his voice even more thunderous. "And *move* it! Move your asses!"

As the squad marched out of the induction center and boarded the bus for camp, the sergeant grinned at Jerome. Jerome decided the topkick did not look at all like a red-faced catfish when he smiled. He's beautiful, thought Jerome, and I want to be just like him. Thanks to him, I ain't scared no more. Thanks to him, I've discovered I'm a leader of men.

Nine months later, when his division shipped out to Korea, Jerome was a corporal. In Korea, Jerome Steele, who had never commanded anything more than a bird-dog or a work mule prior to his army days, discovered that when he led the way into combat, his men followed faithfully. By the time Ike stopped the war in '53, the former hayseed was Staff Sergeant Jerome Steele. The lean boy had thickened into muscled manhood. The two rows of ribbons and medals he wore caused nearly every soldier he passed to do a double take. When Jerome's Colonel awarded him one of his several battle stars, the officer said, in front of the entire battalion, "Sergeant Jerome Steele, our country is grateful and fortunate that you were innately anointed with a MacArthuresque ability to inspire others."

Damn right, thought Jerome. When I order my people to do somethin', they do it. On the double.

Thanks to the GI Bill, Jerome enrolled in the University of Texas when his military career ended. Twenty-six at the time, he had known danger, starvation and privation in glacial Asian winters. He had killed. His fellow students, fuzz-faced college boys and carefree college girls, made Jerome feel like a man among children. They amused him. He regarded their academic achievements with the same appreciation one reserves for a pet terrier's tricks. He was not at all self-conscious about his lack of scholastic background, for he did not think that

14

what they knew, compared to what he knew, was important. As for the hypothesizing, theorizing instructors, Jerome quickly felt contempt for these "mumbly eggheads," as he called them. He made life unbearable for his English prof, a timid little aspiring poet, by constantly calling out, "Cain't hear ya. Talk up." He asked embarrassing questions of his social studies instructor, a man who advocated peaceful resistance but who had never had to fight for his life, face-to-face, when attacked by a murderous enemy. During his first month's exposure to an institution of higher learning, Jerome Steele acquired a disdain for academe and academics which would abide with him for life.

He would have left school before the end of his first semester had it not been for Eunice. Eunice Sowers. He had already written to Washington about a small GI loan that would enable him to open a business for which he felt himself suited, such as a gas station or a gun store. But kismet, and an alphabetical seating arrangement, put Steele, J. and Sowers, E. side by side in Geometry 101.

During the very first weeks of class, Jerome noticed that the pretty, dark-haired girl in the seat next to his never took her gaze off him. She's fallen in love with me at first sight, he thought. He was correct.

Although love was alien to him, Jerome was no stranger to intercourse. As he informed his awed college dorm-mates, "I've had me lotsa women. Lotsa farm girls. Animals, too, heh-heh. Country boys grab what's handy. I've done it in sweet East Texas haystacks and smelly Korean hell-holes. I've done it from Houston to Honolulu to Hong Kong to Hokkaido."

But despite Jerome's worldwide experience, no sex partner had ever meant anything to him until he met Eunice.

She was seventeen—a well-read smalltown girl, also a freshman and an art major. She painted in delicate watercolors—outdoor scenes, bowls of fruit on unusual tablecloths, flowers in copper teakettles. Later, Jerome

15

professed a liking for her artistic endeavors, but privately he never understood going to the trouble of painting an object "when a Kodak takes such an accurate pitcher."

He made her on their first date. They did not even perform the ritual of going to the movies first, or having a burger or a coke. Just bang. In the bushes in front of the Texas History Museum. While he was having her, Jerome was very proud of himself. It was an easy conquest.

But Eunice was a virgin. Afterward, when Jerome realized this sensitive, bright girl had chosen him as her knight, had saved the cathedral of her body for him, had freely given him the most precious thing she had to give, he held her and kissed her damp forehead and pulsing temples. Then and there, in the soft dirt, in a clump of crepe myrtle in front of the Texas History Museum, he knew it had not been Eunice who'd surrendered. He'd surrendered. There he was, tenderly holding that dear, vulnerable, darling girl and wanting never to let go of her, ever again.

On Thanksgiving she took him home to meet her papa, who lived in Elroy, Texas, on the edge of the high plains in the westernmost part of the state.

Initially, Jerome disliked both West Texas and Elroy. He and Eunice traveled by train, and the Austin to Fort Worth all-night coach ride was passionate and wild. They necked all the way, with Eunice reaching such sizzling peaks that she whispered to Jerome, "Yes! Yes!" He could have had her on the train seat, sitting in his lap facing him, covered by her spreading peasant skirt, right there in front of God, the conductor and all their fellow passengers. Her panties had been off since Round Rock. But he loved her totally, respected her too much; he saved her from her heat, restrained himself, protected her propriety.

In Fort Worth the tedium began. They changed to an ancient milktrain that zigzagged northwest through

16

the sun-scourged plains on an all-day crawl toward New Mexico. As soon as Jerome heard the names of some of the train stops—Wink, Shallowater, Muleshoe—he guessed correctly what kind of a ride it would be. Still, the vastness of the empty land shocked him. Miles and miles of unrelenting miles and miles. In the army, whenever Jerome had been called upon to cross country, he had hitched rides on air force transports. Never before had he suffered on an oven-like coach for a full day; he groaned from dusty town to dusty town. He watched balefully as runty mesquites, dead sage, rocks and sand slowly passed his window in eternal procession. The cattle he saw, one to every five acres, were, to his expert eye, the scrungiest, mangiest livestock he'd ever observed. Every few miles, the barbed-wire fence was draped with a coyote carcass, a warning by the ranchers for the dead animal's brethren to keep out.

Near sundown, at the Elroy depot, Jerome decided on first sight that Eunice's home town was no different from Wink, Shallowater and Muleshoe. Her papa met them in a brand new Caddy El Dorado, however, and Jerome's natural gregariousness quickly regenerated itself. When Eunice introduced her two men to each other, the chemistry seemed perfect. Jerome called Mr. Sowers "Papa Sowers"; Papa Sowers called Jerome "son." As they drove up to the Sowers' abode, Jerome suddenly loved West Texas. The house was a substantial two-story brick that squatted regally on one of the few green plots in Elroy.

Next day, as they enjoyed the ritual turkey and cranberries, Papa Sowers asked Jerome all about Korea. Eunice's father had been too young to fight the Kaiser in 1917, too old to personally avenge Pearl Harbor in 1941, and he said that, aside from his wife's early death, these two missed adventures were the major regrets of his life. The old man was fascinated by war and would have made Jerome talk of battle all day had it not been for the annual Texas-Texas A&M game on tv at three o'clock.

17

As the teams were being introduced, Papa Sowers told Jerome all about himself and Eunice. Eunice was an only child. Her mother had died ten years ago. Since then, Papa Sowers' life had orbited around two cherished planets—his daughter Eunice and his thriving automobile agency. By the end of the first quarter, Jerome had captured both of Papa Sowers' cherished planets as easily as he had thrust through Eunice's hymen in the crepe myrtle before the Texas History Museum.

By the time the Longhorns had two second-quarter touchdowns, it was agreed that Jerome and Eunice would wed at Christmas. The couple would live in Elroy, in the two-story brick with Papa Sowers. And Jerome would enter the auto agency as Papa Sowers' eventual half-partner, and take over the business entirely when Papa Sowers retired in a few years.

Poor Papa Sowers retired much earlier than any of them anticipated. It happened a few months after the wedding. The old man woke one morning complaining, "Ah cain't seem to pee none." That night he was dead of uremic poisoning.

It took Eunice months to recover from the shock of her papa's sudden passing. Jerome babied and gentled her with bucolic patience, born of nursing ailing animals in his youth. His patience was sweetened, however, by great love. He adored her in every way, and she knew it. By their first wedding anniversary, he had her smiling and normal again.

The day Papa Sowers' will was read was another milestone in Jerome's life. The old man's death had truly saddened him. He and Papa Sowers had been more than in-laws. During their brief friendship there had been an easygoing role reversal, in which battle-hardened Jerome was the sage and old man Sowers sat wide-eyed at his knee. At times, they had been like brothers. The old man had taken care, when teaching Jerome the auto agency business, never to penalize him for his lack of

18

mercantile background. Jerome felt the loss of his father-in-law deeply.

But when the lawyer's creaky voice intoned the terms of the will, Jerome's sadness was engulfed in tidal waves of jubilation. He hid his joy, of course. But inwardly he reasoned, "Hell, why should I feel guilty because I'm happy. It wasn't me who stopped up his bladder so's he couldn't pee. God stopped it up. Anyway, all this woulda been mine sooner or later. God decided 'sooner,' not me."

Papa Sowers' will had several tingling surprises in it for Jerome. There were, as expected, the two-story brick house, the auto agency and a tidy bank account. But the industrious old man also owned a couple of nice insurance policies naming Eunice and Jerome as beneficiaries, a modest portfolio of hot stocks and several tracts of five-bucks-an-acre West Texas Land. A new chapter began in Jerome's life. Now, to accompany his leadership qualities, he had possessions to match—cash in the bank, a home, a business, land. Respect. Status. Power.

As the aged lawyer read the will, Jerome began to weep, then to sob uncontrollably. Eunice, thinking her husband was lamenting her father's death, was hysterically grateful. She was at the nadir of her despair, yet she had never loved Jerome more than that day when they wailed together in the barrister's office—not knowing that her gratitude was based on a partial truth. Jerome was, indeed, sad about their loss. But he cried that day principally for the same reason a newborn baby cries. That day, as the mantle of wealth wafted down upon him, Jerome felt himself reborn.

By the time Eunice became pregnant with Henry in 1958, four years later, Jerome had used his inspirational ability and inherited wealth to conquer the willing town of Elroy. He was elected president of the chamber of commerce. He won a seat on the school board by telling the voters, "I not only was raised on the three r's, but the three p's—plowin', plantin' n' pickin'. I don't hold with some o' what they'se teachin' kids nowadays, like sex n' anti-Christian philosophies. The bible says, 'Too much learnin' doth make thee mad!' " Soon after, he became a church deacon. He was chosen county chairman of the "Democrats for Ike and Dick in '56." On election night, Jerome and Eunice threw a wingding victory bash to celebrate Ike's carrying Elroy, 342 to 7, over the man Jerome called, "that mumbly college perfesser, Stevenson."

The United States congressman from their district was Jerome's first-name buddy. Jerome's regular hunting partners were the mayor of Elroy, the county sheriff and Reverend Wells of Elroy's largest house of worship. On one occasion, when this prestigious group brought back a boar from a Big Bend safari, they were humorously referred to by the speaker of a rotary luncheon as the "boarsome foursome." But they hunted anything. Quail. Mule deer. Dove. Rabbit. Anything that moved. Jerome, of course, was the best shot, but Reverend Wells was only a millimeter behind.

The president of the Elroy bank came to Jerome's home to personally give him investment advice over a Saturday evening barbecue. Jerome built a warehouse and a motel, drilled for oil on his own land; he razed the corrugated auto agency building Papa Sowers had built in 1934, and erected in its stead a gleaming showroom with a square-block repair department, the largest such building between Lamesa and Vernon.

One Sunday morning in church, from the pulpit, Reverend Wells cited examples of rectitude to Elroy's young and pointed to Jerome as a man they might do well to emulate. Eunice was so proud.

Love-making was organic to their existence. They "did it"—Jerome's term—virtually every time they touched each other. Dinner after dinner was relegated to a burnt destiny in Eunice's oven because when Jerome came home in the evening from work, he and Eunice

20

could not wait until bedtime to do it. They did it anywhere, anytime. Some days, in mid-afternoon, when Jerome felt the energy building up inside him to the point of explosion, he phoned Eunice at home; she would come to the agency and they would do it in Jerome's office on his new Kroehler sofa. Driving home, they might do it on the warm earth behind a butte near the highway. At home, they did it on the floor, on the kitchen table. In the shower. Or the tub. Once, after a few beers, they did it in the basement on Jerome's new pool table, but only once; Eunice forgot to remove her shoes and her spiked heels put two $180 gashes in the felt.

Eunice was his staff and his rock in both their business and their political life. She joined clubs, chaired committees, made speeches, sponsored benefits, gave teas. When Jerome was away looking after their mushrooming properties and interest, she ran the auto agency. Although she was a shy and artistic young woman, she had grown up in her father's business, and actually knew more about it than Jerome. But when she redecorated their house, an incident occurred which was to convince Jerome that Eunice was truly happy with her life, that she was "with" him, all the way.

On the walls of his house—halls, living room, dining room, bedrooms, in every chamber—Papa Sowers had hung all the watercolors Eunice had painted during high school and her half-year of college. The elaborately framed pictures had given incalculable pleasure to the old man. Wherever he looked, there was a reflection of his child's soul. When Papa Sowers died, Eunice and Jerome felt it would be disrespectful, almost sacriligious, to rearrange the house or remove the watercolors. But the paintings made Jerome uncomfortable. He neither liked nor understood their dainty, pastel delicacy, subconsciously regarding them, as well as Eunice's paintbox and easel, as symbols of a part of her he could never infiltrate and subdue. Whenever the muse inspired Eunice to set up her easel and daub a bit, Jerome would

21

only pass through the room in which she worked; he would not remain there. Whenever he watched tv or dined, he always positioned his chair so that no painting was in his line of sight.

As their standing in the community demanded more entertaining at home, Eunice inevitably wanted her own imprint on her own house. She began to replace the things her mother and father had bought twenty years earlier. She bought carpets, drapes, furniture. She re-painted the woodwork. Finally, she re-papered the walls. In the process, the watercolors naturally came down. This inspired no feeling, one way or another, in Jerome. He assumed that after the walls were re-done, the watercolors would be returned to their former hooks all over the house.

He was wrong. He came home from work one Saturday evening and saw, in place of the watercolors, a panorama of prints by the French impressionists. He was agog at the sudden beauty of his house. Every picture matched the furniture, the drapes, the carpets. Not one object in any room was not color-coordinated with any other object.

He walked from print to print, beaming. Eunice followed, basking in his pleasure. "Van Gogh," he read. "Manet." (He pronounced it Minette.) "Them fellas, I hearda them. They got big reputations. Musta cost a lot."

"Not that much. They're prints."

"Oh. I still like 'em."

She smiled.

"Where'dja get 'em?"

"I ordered them. From the Sears catalogue. The frames, too."

"Well, I like 'em." His antennae were out. He did not want to hurt her. "Uh, not as much as whatchoo drew with your watercolor paints." He watched her. "But I like 'em. You got real good taste."

"Thank you, J'rome."

22

He put his arms around her, twirled her, kissed her. She hugged his neck tightly.

"Tomorrow mornin', will you help me with somethin'?" she asked.

"You name it, you got it, sugar pie."

"That ol' wooden boxful of paints and brushes, and that big clumsy easel. They're takin' up too much room in the hall closet. Easel falls every time I open the closet door. Since I'm so busy with meetin's and helpin' you out down at the place, I might as well put that junk up in the attic, out of the way."

He tried to read her mind with his eyes. All he saw was her open, honest face.

"You sure?"

"J'rome, I'm sure, darlin'. Paintin'. I don't have time for that kind of foolishness anymore."

Next morning they pulled down the ladder that led up into the attic. She handed him the wooden box of paints and brushes, then brought the easel up herself as he neatly made a place for her paraphernalia. When he had finished stowing away the symbols of the one misty barrier that had ever separated them, they made love, right there in the attic on top of an old trunk. As Jerome said a couple of months later, "I reckon that was the day I planted Henry inside ya, honey bunch. But I cain't be sure, 'cause we did it so often."

Jerome's imprecision as to the date of Henry's conception notwithstanding, the facts of that winter of '58 were these: Jerome and Eunice were happy and in love; they were wealthy; they were successful; their life was full and rewarding.

And, best of all, of course, Henry was coming.

II

The worst and best year of her life was 1958. In the spring of that year her family doctor said the most beautiful words she had ever heard. He said, "Well, Eunice Sowers Steele, looks like you're goin' to have a baby."

Jerome spent that entire weekend alternately waiting on her and putting his ear to her stomach. She told him it was too early to hear or feel anything, but if Jerome wanted to hear or feel something, he heard it and he felt it. He kept saying, "I feel him, Eunice! I feel him! Right there!"

"Him?" she laughed.

"Him," he said. Not an iota of doubt softened the gruffness in his voice. Even when Jerome was at his tenderest, he barked his words like a deep-throated mastiff. "S'gonna be a him. A *Henry*. After my great grand-daddy. He come to East Texas from Georgia. More'n a hundred years ago. He broke land that'd never been plowed afore. I was raised on that there land." He searched her face. "Henry okay with you?"

Eunice looked down at her still-flat stomach and said, "Hello, Henry."

He laughed. They kissed.

"I'll getcha some iced tea," he shouted, and was gone before she could say she didn't want any. In the two days since the evening she had told him she was pregnant, he had brought her at least a dozen glasses of iced tea.

24

He's so dear, and strong, she thought. Like a force of nature. One minute he shines on you and warms your soul; next minute he blows you over, like a blue norther out of Oklahoma.

She worshipped him. But in years to come she would often forget how much she loved him those years before Henry was born.

Also in 1958, during the second Eisenhower recession, Jerome and Eunice went bankrupt.

That summer, that dusty, choking, terrible summer, they lost everything. Everything. Had Jerome not been such a fighter, they would have at least held on to the house Papa Sowers left them. Under the bankruptcy laws, the court could not have touched their paid-for home. But Jerome had begun to do his own financing a couple of years earlier. In late spring, because of the horrible economic conditions, a host of his credit customers could not meet their payments. Some of them went under leaving Jerome with a safe full of worthless paper. These disasters, coupled with a few dry oil wells Jerome had drilled on his five-bucks-an-acre land, and with buildings he had built and was still paying for, meant that Eunice and Jerome were suddenly out of cash and credit. And friends. The bank president, who had eaten Jerome's barbecue in their backyard while giving advice on how to expand, now told Jerome he was overextended and undercapitalized. When Jerome sought the money-lender's help, he was lectured, then shunted to a vice-president in charge of auto and vacation loans, then shunned altogether. So Jerome set about raising "fightin' money," as he termed it. He sold their stocks at substantially below what Papa Sowers had paid for them, cashed in insurance policies, sold the land for half its purchase price. Finally, he mortgaged the house.

In July, Jerome was forced to file for bankruptcy.

As Eunice blossomed with child during later summer and early fall, Jerome almost ceased to function as a human being. He withdrew into his own world of stunned disbelief, paralyzed by the shock of what had happened to his empire.

In her mind, Eunice could not help comparing the new Jerome to a hound dog she had owned as a child. Her folks had given her the pup for Christmas. A year or so later she left it with a neighbor who owned a ranch, while she and her parents went on a two-week vacation to Galveston. A ranch-hand who hated pet dogs cornered Eunice's pup during her absence and whipped it nearly to death. That summer of her pregnancy, rummaging through one of her schoolgirl scrapbooks, she found the childhood poem she had written about her dog.

Once I had a dog named Flea,
The liveliest little dog you ever did see;
Now, my Flea's just a scared old hound,
His tail between his legs, his head hanging down.

They could not meet the August mortgage payment on Papa Sowers' house, and the bank took the two-story dwelling from them. Mercifully, an old Sowers' family friend owned a tiny old frame house in the center of Elroy and allowed Eunice and Jerome to rent it on credit until Jerome found work.

The little house was on a corner. In its small backyard sat a one-car garage connected to the street by a narrow concrete driveway. The street side of the house faced a block-square park that sported a cracked cement tennis court, a few horseshoe pits, a World War I cannon whose muzzle faced the blacktop highway through town, and a few struggling trees that nearly died every summer when the West Texas sun got at them. Eventually, because Henry was born in it, Eunice came to love that little house. Though its shiplap walls sagged and waved, the outside was whitewashed, the inside was freshly papered, and the roof did not leak during the April gulley-washers. In fact, the little house looked

26

much younger than it was. But its new master, thirty-two-year-old Jerome, looked old and empty.

He found work. Another old friend of Papa Sowers owned what had once been a rival to Jerome's automobile agency. The elderly man graciously gave Jerome a job selling used cars, used trucks and used farm machinery on commission, despite the fact that a few years earlier Jerome had nearly driven his new employer out of business.

The last few months that Eunice carried Henry, they came close to not having enough to eat. Some of their new neighbors, poor folk all, gave them produce from their gardens. Old friends of Eunice's family brought her cooked dishes. The kindly owner of the Elroy Variety Store gave Eunice a part-time job, but after one week her doctor ordered her to quit and stay off her feet as much as possible. The doctor looked after her lovingly —he had brought Eunice into the world himself, twenty-three years earlier—and would take no money for his services. The food, the job, the medical attention were out and out charity, and ordinarily, she would never have considered accepting any of it. But inside her body, her precious baby nestled. As Jerome slipped away from her, as their love dried up like a West Texas creek in a drought, all she thought about was having a healthy child.

Henry was born in October.

He was a gentle, happy baby, born laughing, a great-eyed, darling little boy whose sweetness danced forth from huge, grayblue irises. From the moment she first held him, Henry saved Eunice's life. Jerome did not come into her bedroom to see her or his newborn son. Eunice did not care. She felt her warm, wonderful child in her arms, the hot, new life against her chest, and all she cared about was Henry.

For the first two years of Henry's life, Jerome did not speak to Eunice. The young titan who had planted Henry inside her had become, by the time his seed ripened and his son arrived, a self-pitying, frightened strawman with barely enough courage to rise and go to work each day.

He hated himself, hated living. And one day, about a month before Henry was born, Eunice discovered that Jerome now hated her as well. Perhaps she reminded him of his halcyon years; perhaps, in his irrational mind, she was a symbol of his failure. Eunice could only guess, for Jerome would not talk. Nonetheless, before that particular day, she tried, truly and valiantly tried, to reach him. She spoke to him often and lovingly, even though she knew there would be no answer. She touched him, kissed his cheek, the top of his head. Sometimes he responded by nodding or grunting. Sometimes he sighed. Occasionally he rose and left the room. But on this day, he pushed her away. Hard. Angrily. She nearly fell. She might have lost her baby. From that day on, she never kissed him again.

After Henry came, Jerome paid his wife and son no mind, and they paid him very little. When Henry began to crawl, then walk, Eunice always made sure the baby never approached Jerome—though the child might as well have been invisible, judging by how much attention the distraught father paid his son.

Eunice kept house and cooked. Jerome went to work each morning, came home each night, ate in silence, listened to the radio or watched tv—or seemed to—then went to bed soon after on the living-room sofa. Eunice slept in the cottage's one bedroom, where Henry's crib was. Every Saturday night, Jerome put his wages on the kitchen table for Eunice to look after. On Sundays, Jerome and Eunice acted as if the other did not exist.

Repeatedly, Eunice thought to herself: All I can say about this bitter, strange man is that he hasn't run off from us, he doesn't drink, and he lives like a monk.

The pall that saturated their home lifted each weekday morning when Jerome left for work. The house brightened, the sun came out. Henry and Eunice ate together, cleaned together, laundered together, shopped together.

They sang, they strolled, they mud-pied, chattered, gardened, gathered acorns, peeped down prairie-dog holes. Henry was an affectionate baby. He loved to touch Eunice, for her to touch him. They kissed and cuddled.

Manly laughs came from his little gut, infectious, totally delighted. He laughed often and Eunice laughed with him.

One day in the variety store, Eunice lingered over a box of cheap watercolors. She had not thought of painting for years. Her old wooden box of paints and brushes, her old easel, had been washed away, along with everything else, in the riptide of bankruptcy. For six weeks she did without tea and cokes, saving enough to buy not only the watercolors for herself, but a box of Crayolas for Henry and drawing paper for both of them. Thereafter, mother and son daubed and scrawled whenever they felt like it. Her work was precise, delicate and disciplined, but Henry's two-year-old's slashes and scribblings were formless, uninhibited, funny. When he found he could make her laugh with his creations, they became madder and madder. He would not consider a picture finished and ready for presentation until he had used all six colors in his Crayola box and covered every square inch of the paper with squiggles and swirls.

During those first two years of Henry's life, Eunice refused to acknowledge Jerome's obvious mental breakdown. She lived totally within herself and Henry. And therein in a schizophrenic way she was happier than she had been before the bankruptcy, happier than she had been as a child. However, as she told a friend years later, "I hadn't learned my lesson about happiness. Bein' a West Texas gal, I should've known that anythin' lovely and delicate and alive, things like yucca blooms, things like happiness, are mortal. The desert heat gets at flowers; human nature gets at happiness. If you want to treasure beauty, engrave it in your memory while you're seein' or feelin' it. Then, when beauty dies, at least you have the remembrance of it inside you."

Just after Henry's second birthday, Jerome began to take Eunice's son away from her. The process took ten years, and Eunice was so unaware and unsuspecting that it took five of those years before she realized that Jerome had Henry's life under siege. By the time she awakened to the danger, Eunice had as much chance of winning him back from Jerome's hegemony as an armless man does of winning a wrestling match.

It began with a lawn sprinkler. A simple lawn sprinkler. It was on an October day in 1960. Eunice was washing the dinner dishes. Outside, daylight lingered. Henry played in the backyard, and Jerome sat on the back steps, staring at everything, seeing nothing. Or so Eunice thought.

She did not hear Jerome come into the kitchen. Since the bankruptcy, he had a way of moving around the house like an odorless, gray vapor. Eunice seldom heard him come or go; she had to be looking at him to know he was there. This particular day, however, she sensed his presence and turned. There he was, standing in the doorway between the kitchen and back porch, looking at her. She stared back at him and waited.

He cleared his throat. "Come on out here for a minute." These were the first words he had spoken to her since before Henry was born.

Jerome talked at work, of course, but as little as possible, and the townsfolk, knowing who he had been and what he had endured, put up with his brutal frankness. In a perverse way, Jerome's use of the truth to flay his listeners actually kept the Steeles from starving. The ranchers and farmers knew Jerome would always tell them exactly what was wrong with a used vehicle or piece of farm equipment. "This pickup's a pile o' rusty crud," he'd growl. Or, "This here reaper ain't worth cow chips." Increasingly, his customers trusted him, so that when he grumbled, "This heap'll run fairly good if you get the owner of this two-bit outfit to put in a new drive shaft afore you putcha money down," they believed him, and bought from him.

But he never spoke to Eunice at home. Now, here he was, asking her to come outside.

"What is it?" she asked.

He turned, went out, and stood on the back steps, staring at Henry playing in the backyard grass.

Eunice followed Jerome outside and for a puzzled minute stood beside him, alternately looking at him and then at the target of his fascination—Henry, playing with the lawn sprinkler.

"What is it?" she said again. "If you don't want the baby to play with that thing, tell him to stop. Or I'll tell him. He plays with it all the time."

Jerome stared at her as if she were blind. "Just look," he said.

Again, Eunice looked at Henry. This time she saw what Jerome saw. It was amazing.

The lawn sprinkler had three arms on it. At the end of each arm were water-holes. When the water was on, the pressure of the liquid coursing through the hose and out the water-holes caused the arms to rotate so fast they could hardly be seen.

Now, however, the water was off and little Henry sat with his legs spread wide, the lawn sprinkler on the grass between them. The child's game consisted of grasping one of the sprinkler arms in a small hand, deftly whirling it so fast that the arms rotated in a blur, looking down at the blur and—flick!—catching two of the sprinkler arms in each of his unbelievably quick hands, as cleanly as a toad's tongue captures a fly in flight. While his parents stood and watched, the absorbed baby performed his feat unerringly, time after time. Spin. Catch. Spin. Catch. So rapt was the child's concentration that he was unaware of their presence. His gray-blue eyes never left the spinning sprinkler.

Jerome whispered, "I tried it myself. Couldn't even do it once. When I reached in to catch them arms, they bumped my fingers ever'time. He catches it clean. Ever-time." Henry did it again. Spin. Catch. "Catches it clean as a whistle. Ever' blamed time!"

Eunice gaped at her husband. When Elijah first saw the chariot of fire, she thought, he must've looked like Jerome does right now. Never saw a man so taken.

Searching for a way to continue the conversation, she said stupidly, "That's cute, J'rome."

"Cute?" He took his eyes off Henry just long enough to wither her with a glance. "I never seen coordination like that in mah life. Hands n' eyes. Workin' perfect together. I never seen reactions like that there boy's got."

Sudden anger drove her to snap, "That there boy, as you call him, has a name. His name is Henry, J'rome." The pain in his gray face silenced her. She hated herself for an instant. Jerome had spoken to her. The Lord only knew what torment he had overcome in order to finally break his silence, to share this moment with her. And here she was about to drive him away again. His eyes—they were the same color as Henry's—told her he was sorry.

She smiled at him. For a moment the muscles in both their necks tightened, their throats ached, they could not swallow. They fought hot tears. And then he forced himself to smile back, a rusty, aching smile.

Jerome went out in the yard and sat in the grass next to Henry, who stopped playing and studied his daddy. It was the first time Jerome had ever displayed human interest in his son. Confused, the child looked to his mother. Jerome gently reached into the baby's lap and twirled the sprinkler arms. Henry's eyes went from the sprinkler to Jerome's face and back again to the sprinkler. And back to Jerome's face. Suddenly, the little boy laughed, delighted with his burly new playmate. Henry peered down at the blur in his lap, intent as a chickenhawk upon a hen, then—flick!—his small hands shot out and caught two of the sprinkler arms with absolute precision. Henry laughed again. Jerome laughed and ruffled his son's hair.

Eunice went back into the house and stuffed a dishtowel against her mouth to keep them from hearing her

32

sobs. For another half-hour, as she peeped at them through the kitchen window, Jerome and Henry played their silly game with the sprinkler. She wept the entire time. No one heard; no one knew.

They've found each other, she thought. I'm so happy. Maybe now Jerome and I will be like we were.

As she admitted later she had not learned her lesson about happiness.

A couple of months after the lawn-sprinkler incident, Jerome brought Henry an armful of cheap dime-store games of skill for Christmas. A set of small bowling pins with a plastic ball. Tiddlywinks. A junky little pinball machine. A child's oilcloth-covered punching bag that stood on one flexible metal leg connected to a masonite base; the light bag, when struck, bounced to the floor, then came swiftly up again. A clown's face inside a round glass-topped case. Where there should have been eyes and teeth, the clown's face had holes, and the tiny steel balls in the case had to be rolled around until all the holes were filled.

Henry was delirious with excitement. He adored games, perhaps because he was unbelievably skillful at them. It took him less than twenty seconds to fill the clown's eyes and teeth with the steel balls. Each time he swung at the bouncing punching bag, he connected solidly with his small fists. At first Eunice was unimpressed with this feat, until Jerome bellowed at his uncomprehending wife, "Okay, then, *you* try it, Eunice." She tried it. Several times she missed completely, and when she did manage to connect with the-swooping bag, it was only glancingly. From that moment, she looked at her manchild with the knowledge that his reflexes were prodigious.

She realized that Henry was extraordinary in another way, too. His attention span was phenomenal. The child never seemed to be bored. Hour after hour, he would play with his tiddlywinks, snapping one colored button after another into the plastic cup. Seldom missing. When

33

he did miss, she noticed, he would try the muffed shot again and again, until he hit five, ten times in a row. Only then would he shoot from another distance.

And when Jerome was nearby, Eunice saw, Henry would look at his daddy after each try, as if success was meaningless without his daddy's smile of approval.

Basketball.

When he had mastered all the store-bought games Jerome brought home, the child created games. One Saturday night, when Henry was only five, he and Jerome watched a basketball game on tv. When it was over, Henry found a wire clothes hanger, bent it into a circle, closed his bedroom door, climbed up on a chair, and jammed the hook part of the hanger tightly into the crack at the top so that the newly formed hoop stuck out. For a basketball, that first day, the child took an odd sock of his daddy's and stuffed it tightly with newspaper. Later, he shot anything he could get his chubby hands on through that hanger hoop: oranges, old tennis balls, marbles, acorns, paper grocery bags crumpled into balls.

Jerome watched Henry's addiction to the hoop without comment, listened silently to the tales Eunice related about Henry's daily, virtually nonstop basketball game at the bedroom door. One Saturday, a few weeks later, Jerome came home from work with a large mail-order carton from Sears. In the box were an honest-to-goodness backboard, a basket and a basketball.

When Eunice came home from church the next morning, the backboard and basket were mounted over the entrance to the garage. They are still there.

Why basketball? Why not baseball, or football, or track?

It could very easily have been baseball, but Jerome had an argument with Henry's little league coach. When Henry was eight he tried out for the Elroy little league

34

team, even though all the other boys were from ten to twelve years of age.

Henry's first day out, the coach made him the team's pitcher. Jerome and Henry were elated. At dinner that night, for the first time in years, Jerome chatted cheerfully. Slowly and painfully, he was shaking off the humiliation of going under, was becoming a human being again. He still did not talk much, never showed open affection to Eunice or Henry; he still slept on the sofa. But Jerome doted on his son. He played catch with him for hours, or watched him shoot baskets all day on a Sunday, participated in just about any silly game Henry devised—throwing pennies into coffee cups, or crumpled paper balls into an ashcan. And if Jerome was not warm to Eunice, at least he was no longer hostile. Those were pleasant years for her; there was peace in the house. But she was unaware that she was losing her son.

The trouble began when the little league coach tried to teach Henry to throw a curveball. The child had already delighted the coach with his fastball, as well as all the old-timers who gathered those pleasant April afternoons at the red clay diamond to watch the children work out.

And then Jerome's best, and only, friend came to one of the work-outs. The man, aside from being the town drunkard, was a part-time mechanic at the auto agency where Jerome sold used vehicles. In his youth, Jerome's friend had been a baseball pitcher of talent, enough to earn him a contract with the White Sox. When he observed the little league coach teaching eight-year-old Henry how to throw a curve, the sot sought out Jerome, pulled him aside and whispered fervently, "See what that fool is doin' to your boy? Curveballs!"

He shook Jerome to emphasize each bourbon-tainted word. "Don't let your younker throw no curveballs!" he grated. "Not 'til he's growed up and his bones is strong and set! I ruined my arm with curveballs, J'rome! Tha's why I ain't in the Bigs right now! Curveball's what did it! They'll ruin your boy's arm for sure! For always!"

Jerome marched onto the field, placed himself between his startled, wide-eyed son and the coach, and barked, "I don' wan' Henry here throwin' none o' them curveballs."

"Why not, Mr. Steele?" the surprised coach asked.

"Don' make no diff'rence why not."

"Well, lookee here, Mr. Steele, I'm the coach of this team, and—"

"You gonna teach Henry to throw a curveball?"

"Well, sir, I might not, or I might. What I'd like to find out from you is what—"

"Come on, Henry," Jerome said.

He led the now solemn child off the field. At age eight, Henry Steele said goodbye to baseball.

When Henry was nine, he went out for peewee football. And, yes, the coach made Henry his quarterback immediately. Henry could pass a football thirty yards right through a tire hanging from a tree limb, and he was so shifty of foot, possessed such a good sense of balance, that he was hard to tackle. Jerome knocked off work to watch the peewee team's first scrimmage of the season. Henry was tackled on an early play and another young player accidentally stomped on his hand. Jerome marched into the field, examined his son's superficial cut, wrapped the hand in his kerchief, and led Henry off the field and away from football forever.

As for track, Henry simply did not run that fast. He was fast, but not blindingly fast. His strengths were quickness, finesse, precision, brains. He could fake and feint. He could throw a ball and hit what he meant to hit. His hands, his feet, his entire body coordinated with his eyes and mind.

In short, one game in particular was his destiny.

Basketball.

A week or so after Jerome aborted Henry's football career, he bought a book, written by a famous coach and published by a sports magazine, on how to play basketball.

The book was written like a military manual, complete with detailed instructions and step-by-step drawings, diagrams, charts and photographs.

Every week Jerome and Henry took up a different page. How to dribble. How to pass. How to rebound. How to shoot free throws. Jump shots. Hook shots. How to hold your wrist, your elbow, your shoulder. How to pivot. How to cut. Set a pick. A screen. How to weave. Glide. Drive the baseline. Press.

The book was like a foreign language to Eunice when she rifled through it, but it was like a bible to her two men. Their basketball "court," the driveway in the backyard, was the crossroad of her activities as she traversed her domain—from clothesline to garbage cans to garden, from lawntending to gossiping over the back fence. Her kitchen window was a ringside seat overlooking the "court." Even in her living room and bedroom, as she watched tv or tried to lose herself in a library book, the resounding thump-thump-thump of the dribbled basketball jarred her. The scrapes and squeaks of Henry's sneakers as he cut and pivoted grated her spine and made goosebumps on her skin, the sudden *woinggggg* of the ball hitting the basket's rim echoed inside her head.

Yet she took pleasure in what Jerome and Henry were doing. Now the Steeles were a family. Her husband and son had this strong bond between them, a cause in common. When Jerome was home the house was no longer oppressive with hate. The place buzzed with energy, with activity.

She even took pleasure in the uncanny hold Jerome had over Henry. Though at times it hurt her feelings that the child treasured one small nod from his daddy more than all her loving hugs and kisses, she rationalized by thinking it was because she had always approved of everything Henry did, while Jerome approved of perfection only. How that boy wants to please his daddy! she thought. The week Henry and Jerome undertook the left-handed dribble, Henry spent four hours every day after school for five days, plus all day Satur-

37

day—almost thirty relentless hours of thump-thump-thump—just to show Jerome on Sunday morning how perfectly he had mastered bouncing a ball with his left hand. When Jerome reacted to Henry's proud demonstration with a small smile and nod, Eunice thought the boy looked as if he had just found the golden grail.

As Eunice told her neighbor one day over the back fence, "when I hear on the radio and tv about those hippies burnin' and riotin' on the streets of Chicago durin' the Democratic convention, and cursin' at the police, and takin' dope, and despisin' their parents, I thank God Henry is the way he is. My son might be only ten, but it's easy to see he loves his daddy and would never hurt him. Always honor and obey him. And, after all, what more can any mama want of her son?"

By 1970, however, when Henry was twelve, Eunice was sincerely convinced that both her husband and son were mentally ill. Basketball had become their obsession. It was seemingly all they lived for, spoke about, thought about. In every kind of weather, there was Henry after school, dribbling and shooting in their back-yard driveway, going one-on-one with anyone who would play him. In the evenings, when Jerome came home from work, he would sit on the back porch, over-coated in winter, short-sleeved in summer, and watch his son practice. Occasionally, Jerome would position himself where Henry requested so the boy could practice rebounding. Jerome's height advantage was invaluable to the twelve-year-old Henry, who would strain and stretch to jump higher than his father could reach flatfooted.

The cold war between Eunice and Jerome over Henry ended and the hot war began one freezing February afternoon. On that day she nagged Henry into coming indoors and forsaking his basketball practice. When Jerome came home that night, Eunice defiantly informed him that it was too cold for the boy to be outdoors.

Jerome's reaction confirmed Eunice's feelings about his mental state. He was furious. He scolded her in front of the child the way he had once dressed down city-born Army privates. Eunice fought back, expressing her doubts about Jerome's sanity, her fears about his influence on Henry's normality.

Henry had never before seen or heard his parents quarrel. The child's frightened eyes brimmed with tears.

"Honest, Ma, I'll wear warm clothes. Please let me practice," he said.

Eunice relaxed her bantam-rooster stance and knelt before the child to reason with him. But one glance at his pleading grayblue eyes and she knew she might as well try to reason with a shot deer.

"I'll wear mittens, Ma," Henry sniffled, sensing victory.

She hugged and kissed him. "You promise?"

"Oh, yes'm."

She knew that if she fought further she would lose more than the battle. Her son's love was at stake.

"All right. If you wear mittens."

Henry gave her the sweetest hug he had given her in years.

And Henry did wear mittens when he practiced basketball outdoors. He wore them all winter, everytime he played. He wore them all summer as well. That was because Henry and Jerome had heard a basketball star say in a tv interview that playing basketball with gloves on gives a player a "feel" for the ball, an ability to control it by balance and the ball's own momentum, rather than by tactile adhesion. It was said, years later, that Henry's practicing with mittens on was instrumental in making him the best ballhandler ever to play Texas high-school basketball.

That was Eunice's only contribution ever to his career.

And so, in that year of 1970, the loving, reflective Eunice began her steady descent into sullen shrewishness. Her mien turned tense, wary, nervous; the soft voice hardened into either studied flatness or an angry whine. Slowly, undeniably, Eunice became Mrs. Bad around the house and, as she curdled, Jerome became Mr. Good.

Jerome continued to drive Henry without respite, and Eunice angrily saw that the consumed boy had neither time nor energy for school, friends and church. She and Jerome fought constantly. Her vitriol was more obvious than his because she knew her cause was doubly without hope. She knew that if she won over Jerome, she was in danger of losing Henry's love. Basketball was, by then, the boy's staff of life. But she loved the child, wanted more than "just" basketball for him. She hated Jerome. She wanted to punish him for stealing her son. For stealing her youth.

She was only thirty-four. Despite the hard set of her face, she was prettier than she had ever been. She had filled out in all the right places; the thin, doll-like college girl Jerome had wed was now a full-breasted, thin-waisted, head-turning woman. When she walked in public, men looked at her. Sometimes their unspoken askings set her to burning inside. She had—had always had—a huge appetite for fleshly desires. Now she tried to repress them, but everyday she ached for a man, shamed herself with her daydreams about every young buck in Elroy.

She never fantasized about Jerome, never thought of him anymore as a man, primarily because he never indicated in any way that he thought of her or wanted her body. Eunice honestly felt that the bankruptcy and the later preoccupation with Henry's basketball had atrophied Jerome's manhood completely. She assumed that he was totally devoid of sexual desires. She was wrong.

On the day of the first public basketball game in which twelve-year-old Henry played, Eunice discovered how wrong she was about Jerome.

It was a Saturday in November, the opening game of the small-fry church league for eleven- to thirteen-year-old boys. The church gym had no grandstands. All

40

twenty-five or so spectators—the families of the children—sat on folding chairs along the sidelines.

Jerome was so nervous for Henry that Eunice actually felt pity for the man. At home during breakfast he had to use both hands in order to get his coffee cup to his lips without spilling it. Henry, on the other hand, was deadly calm.

The game started. The children all looked like Charlie Chaplin in their baggy basketball shorts—except for Henry. Jerome had insisted that Eunice tailor his shorts. Henry looked trim, neat, perfectly built, even though he was one of the shortest boys on the court. But he seemed to have a bearing, a proud quality, that singled him out. Maybe it's the shorts, thought Eunice.

During the first part of the game, Henry seldom got the ball. When he did, he passed it off, crisply and nicely. After a few minutes, with the score nothing to nothing, the coach of Henry's team called time out. As the little boys gathered around their coach, Jerome stood up.

As usual, Henry was watching his daddy, looking for a nod or a smile. Jerome waved for Henry to come over to him. Henry knew it was wrong to leave his coach's huddle, but never, ever did the child disobey Jerome. Henry came over.

"Shoot the ball," Jerome ordered.

Henry blinked. "Sure, Daddy." He took a deep breath and added, "The coach said I should pass it."

"I said, shoot it. Ever'time you get your hands on it. Hear?" Jerome said.

"Yes, sir," Henry whispered.

The first time the ball was passed to Henry, he did what he had done on his back driveway at least ten thousand times over the past seven years. He faked to his right, dribbled behind his back to his left, jumped up in the air and shot. The ball went through the basket without touching the rim. It was so quickly and brilliantly executed, so remarkable an achievement for a twelve-year-old boy, that at first there was silence; then came

41

applause and shouts. It was the first basket of the game. It was the first basket Henry ever scored in a game. It was the beginning of a sports legend in West Texas.

Henry scored thirty-six points that day. His team won the game, 39 to 12. Usually, Eunice had been told, small-fry games had maximum scores of less than twenty points a team. No one boy had ever scored over fourteen points in a small-fry game before. Eunice noted the strange, all-knowing look on Jerome's face when, after Henry's fifth basket, Henry's coach began to shout at his team, "Pass it to Henry!" And when they passed it to Henry, the coach shouted, "Shoot, son, shoot! Shoot, Henry!"

When the game ended, the coach and almost everyone else ran out on the court. The prodigious Henry was carried on jubilant shoulders over to Jerome and Eunice. Congratulations were showered upon them. Eunice was forced to admit to herself that she liked what was happening.

The family celebrated. They walked to the Elroy Cafe and ordered pecan pie, ice cream and milk. Word spread fast in Elroy, and it was as if the Steeles were holding court. Whoever came into the cafe approached them and said nice things. During all this, Henry's face was blank, but his eyes grew bigger and bluer than ever, and a new fire, a fierce and victorious glint, that Eunice had never seen in them before burned happily. Jerome's joy was feverish. Whenever someone said, "I heard young Henry here really tore 'em up today," Jerome babbled, "Yes, *sir*, young Henry here really tore 'em up! Really tore 'em up!"

Eunice felt good. Lord knew, the Jerome Steeles had had little enough to celebrate the past twelve years, and now here they were, center stage, with their neighbors showering compliments. Oh, she still felt that basketball was just a silly game, and that Henry was leading an unbalanced life. She even knew, subconsciously, that the very success she was enjoying at that moment was going to render her defenseless in future battles with Jerome.

42

While she was smiling and saying thank you to all her fellow townspeople, she knew exactly what Jerome would say to her when they got home: "I toldja so, Eunice. Toldja so. All that there work paid off! Now maybe you-all'll get off me n' Henry's back."

It was dark when they reached home. Henry went right to bed, exhausted. When Eunice tucked him in and kissed him goodnight, it was if he could read the confusion in her mind. He hugged her neck a little tighter and longer than usual, as if to say, "Please, Ma. I love you. But I'm on Daddy's side."

She turned off the lights in Henry's room, shut the door and went into the living room. It was empty. She went into her bedroom. He was there, sitting on the bed, looking directly at her in a way he had not looked at her for almost thirteen years.

Her body responded immediately. She felt a hot cloud of excitement explode in her. The cloud spread to her legs, her fingers, tingling her skin, drying her lips. Gooseflesh covered her arms, made her shiver at what was about to happen. In a moment she would be surrounded and taken. Startled, she realized that somewhere, hidden deep, her love for him still lingered.

She barely managed to say, "J'rome?"

"Eunice," he said, "I wantcha to be my wife again."

She did not trust herself to speak for fear she would cry and deflate his desire. When she did not answer, he assumed she was saying no to him.

His voice was husky. "All these years. I—I'm sorry. But I wasn't—I wasn't *worthy* of you, Eunice. I didn't *deserve* to have you. After what I did, losin' ever'thing. But, God, I wanted you! Ever' minute. You follow what I'm sayin'? Y'know how *ashamed* I was? How much I hated myself? How could I ask you to love me, if I hated myself?"

Her back was to him. She unbuttoned the top button of her blouse.

"When I went under," he continued, "I started to kill myself. Y'know why I didn't kill myself, Eunice?"

43

She unbuttoned the second button of her blouse. The fire inside her was roaring; she was at the point of suffocation. She imagined his rough hands on her breasts, his strong lips against her own.

"I needed to be punished. For losin' ever'thing. I didn't kill myself because that would've been the easy way. Livin'! That was the worst punishment I could think of. Livin'! *Facin'* folks. Folks who knew how ignorant and prideful and foolish I'd been. And doin' without you, Eunice. That was my punishment for failin', for losin' ever'thing."

He was almost choking in his effort not to sob. She could hardly wait to hold him, to comfort him. But despite her certain surrender, she was determined that he should make the first move. Oh, if he would only touch her! She would do the rest.

"The night you gave birth," he said, "that night I wasn't worthy of bein' there. You follow what I'm sayin'? I stayed out of your bedroom because I couldn't face you, Eunice. Because—I didn't want my son to see a piece o' crud like me his first night on God's earth."

The bedspring creaked. She knew he had risen, was standing right behind her. She could feel the warmth of his body. She turned and faced him. Deliberately, she took off her blouse.

But he continued to talk. "Now that's all over, though. I'm a man again, Eunice. Because o' Henry!"

Henry!

Once, as a child, she had seen a dog get hung up in a bitch. Her papa had poured ice water over the dogs and the pair "got unhung pronto," as Papa Sowers had put it. She felt as if Jerome had just poured ice water over her. She began putting her blouse back on.

"You want me because of Henry?" she said.

"Y'know what I mean. I've got my self-respect back, Eunice. I've been successful with my son."

Thirteen years of fighting had done terrible things to her. This man had stolen her son. She wanted to hurt him.

44

"All right," she said, "I'll be your wife again. On one condition."

He knew what the condition was, but he whispered anyway, "What?"

"My boy," she shouted. "I want my boy back! I want him to have friends. And study his schoolbooks. And go to church. AND NOT PLAY SO GOD-DAMNED MUCH BASKETBALL! I want my boy to be *normal*! He's only twelve, J'rome! God damn you! I want my boy back!"

She thought he was going to kill her. Really kill her. His bulging eyes went past her for a second, and she knew what he was looking at. He was looking through the doorway, into the livingroom, at the wall over the mantel. A 30-30 Winchester was mounted there.

He killed her in another way. His teeth gnashing, the veins in his neck standing out, he roared, "Not ever, you dumb bitch! He's mine. He's my only reason for livin'. Not ever! Henry ain't makin' the same mistakes in life I made. When my chance come, I wasn't ready. I was ignorant. I wasn't sharp. So they was able to come up behind me and whup me. Well, *Henry's gonna be ready!* YOU HEAR! He ain't gonna be like me! He's gonna *work hard*! God's given him a gift! I'm gonna see to it he uses that there gift to get to the top! And when he gets there, by Jesus, he's gonna stay there! YOU HEAR ME! You get in my way, and I'll—!"

He did not finish. There was no need. She knew what he would certainly do to her and to himself if she got in his way.

He stormed out of her bedroom and never came back again.

The next afternoon Henry came home from school and went straight outside to practice basketball in the driveway. From three to six-thirty. Like a machine, a robot. Fake. Dribble. Jump. Shoot. *Swish!* Fetch the ball. And do it again. And again. She watched him through the window as she prepared dinner.

45

Some children were playing tag across the street in the park, shouting and laughing, unaware of Henry's existence. Through the kitchen window, Eunice saw Henry stop practicing for a moment and stand there, watching the children in the park. He smiled a little as they ran and laughed and enjoyed each other. A quick shadow clouded the boy's face, a hungry, envious look. A lonely look. Then it was gone. Henry's face went blank.

Eunice knew she was right and Jerome was wrong. But when Henry whirled and, like an automaton, returned to his basketball practice, she knew also that no matter how right she was, it was too late. The war was over. She had lost.

Jerome came home at six-thirty. He ignored her.

Just as the sun was about to set, Eunice called through the window, "Henry, come on in the house now, darlin'. It's gettin' late."

She saw Henry relax in the middle of a dribble, take a step toward the house.

"Eunice! The boy is practicin'!"

Jerome rushed past her and snapped on the spotlight he had hung outside so that Henry could practice at night. He stepped out the back door.

"Son!" he barked. "You jus' keep right on. You're doin' fine, Henry!"

Henry stood at attention, smiled back. The night light turned the yard, turned Eunice's entire world, into an eerie, sickly yellow.

Henry faked, dribbled, shot. The ball went in. Jerome gave a deep laugh and came back into the house. He swept through the kitchen without looking at Eunice, went into the living room and turned on the tv. She heard Walter Cronkite. From outside on the driveway, she heard the hollow thump-thump-thump of the basketball, the squeaking and scraping of Henry's sneakers. She felt as if she were going mad.

III

The game had been over for an hour, and the gymnasium was now dark and quiet. The parking lot and nearby streets were bare; the cars and pickups that had gathered from a radius of a hundred miles had dispersed in noisy, bumper-to-bumper confusion. Their heat radiated quickly skyward, leaving the March night cool and empty.

Tonight had been a special night. Tonight had been Henry Steele's last home game as an Elroy High School basketball player. Only the state championship tournament in Austin, nearly three hundred miles away, lay ahead, then his high-school career, the most brilliant in Texas schoolboy basketball history, would be over. And it seemed unlikely that Elroy would ever again spawn a champion of Henry's stature, one who would move West Texans to shake buildings with their roars.

Henry and Chris emerged from a dimly lit back door of the gym and walked through the darkness of the parking lot toward the park across the street. Beyond the small park was Henry's house; two doors beyond was Chris' house. Henry wore his green-and-white Elroy High School letterman's jacket. An army of patches adorned the sleeves and chest of the garment. The patches proclaimed Henry to have been All-District three times, All-State three times, a member of the district championship team three times, a member of the state championship team twice, captain of his team three years, the Most Valuable Player in the state champion-

47

ship tournament two years—and, finally, in proud purple letters on an iridescent gold background, High School All-American, 1975.

"What a game, Henry!" Chris said. "You went out like a lion. Congratulations, man!"

"Thanks." Henry's voice was boyish, but surprisingly deep.

"No, I really mean it! Wow, that one lay-up! You hung in the air for an hour and put the ball behind your back eighty-four times on the way up!"

Henry laughed. Chris' hyperbole was a fact of life in Elroy.

They walked a few steps in silence, each boy retreating into his thoughts.

"Henry?"

"Yeah."

"I'm sorry I popped my cork the other night."

"Hey, it's okay." Henry smiled at his friend. With Chris he was relaxed, a normal young man who smiled and laughed frequently. With others, his sober demeanor was as much a part of him as his letter jacket.

"No, I really mean it! It wasn't your fault. There's no excuse for an infantile tantrum like I threw. It's just that, hell, I found myself trapped in an untenable Kafkaesque dilemma. And like an equine's posterior, I took it out on my *amigo numero uno*."

Henry laughed. Christopher Blair's verbosity was also a notorious fact of life in Elroy, a community whose natives spoke with monosyllabic economy.

"Now what the crud does a . . . uh . . . Kafkaesque whatever-you-said mean?" he asked.

"It means that forces over which I have no control are ruinin' my life, man."

"Oh."

Chris' "infantile tantrum" had occurred two weeks earlier.

That night Henry had phoned Chris around nine

48

o'clock, as soon as he arrived home from his after-dinner basketball practice at the gym.

"Hey, Chrissie, how'ya doin'?"

"I'll get my algebra book and be right there, *amigo numero uno!*"

Henry laughed. "How'd you know what I wanted, man?"

In his most sinister Bela Lugosi voice, Chris intoned, "Is not there an algebra test tomorrow, Hendry Shteele?"

Groucho Marx, W.C. Fields, Dr. Strangelove, Boris Karloff, Mr. Peepers, Donald Duck—Chris' arsenal was considerable and unpredictable. Because he was a brilliant student, his English teacher had once allowed him to continue reciting Hamlet's soliloquy as Woody Woodpecker. Another time he had done the first lines of Beowulf in old English as Porky Pig might have delivered them.

That night, as he had done countless times, Chris came over to prepare his friend for a test. All through junior and senior high school, as Henry's jock-star had risen, Chris alone had kept him from flunking scholastically.

Chris was an intuitive genius in anticipating and encapsulating what subject matter Henry should memorize at the last minute, and coupled with his ability to anticipate the test questions was the fact that he spent as much time studying as Henry spent playing basketball. He was the brightest and best student in Elroy High School, and he took devilish pride in what he and Henry called The Christopher Blair Method—the teaching, by rote, of enough facts to enable Henry to pass.

It helped, of course, that Henry had an adhesive mind. Random facts stuck to his brain as he himself stuck to the man he was guarding on a basketball court. He had no interest whatsoever in what he learned, allowing the material to slip from his mind as soon as he no longer needed it. In fact, Henry was anti-intellectual. He regarded books and data and abstractions as ene-

49

mies to be overcome only in order, as Chris put it, "to obey the commandment, 'Thou Shalt Flunknot.' "

To many people, the deep friendship between these two boys was unlikely. Yet the proximity of their houses and Chris' sensitive, perceptive mind had made him seek out Henry from the time they were in church kindergarten together. As Chris said, "Maybe I made friends with you, Henry, because I've always had a proclivity for the unique, and being little Henry Steele's friend was certainly unique." And perhaps Henry had been so hungry for a friend that sheer loneliness drove him to accept Chris' overtures. Whatever the explanation, the truth was that the two boys had immediately liked the qualities they perceived in each other.

The only major continuing disagreement between Henry and Chris was over the subject of girls. Henry loved sex but hated dating. Whenever Chris asked Henry to double-date with him, the answer was almost always no. When they did go out as a foursome, the evening usually ended with Henry's sullen silence and the girl's near-tears of rejection.

"You go for a chick like most people go for a carwash," Chris once said to Henry. "In and out, and forget it 'til the next time you need it."

By their senior year, Henry had slept with virtually every desirable girl in Elroy High School, but seemed not to like a single one of them. Chris, on the other hand, had charmed his way into an equal number of perfumed panties, and loved them all.

That night in early March, as Chris was coaching Henry in algebra, Jerome burst in on them, brandishing two envelopes.

"Look what come in today's mail! Two more!"

Jerome opened both envelopes, read the letters inside, and handed them to Henry, who scanned them quickly and smiled with pleasure.

"Michigan and Arizona!" Hah!" Jerome shouted. "Put 'em with the others, Henry-boy!"

50

Sheepishly, Henry reached under his bed and pulled out a shoebox that bulged with orderly bundles of letters secured by rubber bands.

"Ain't that somethin', Chris-boy!" Jerome barked. "He's got nearly *two hunderd* of them there ath-a-letic scholarship offers! From the best doggone universities in the U.S. of A!"

To Chris, Henry's father sounded like a lactating cow that had not been milked for a month. Henry did not know it, but Chris had always hated the singleminded, semi-literate Jerome.

With a triumphant laugh, Jerome left the room, slamming the door behind him.

Henry, embarrassed, replaced the shoebox beneath the bed. Never had he mentioned this plethora of scholarship offers to his closest friend, his supposed confidant.

Chris lost his temper. "Fuckin' lousy stinkin' system," he muttered.

"Take it easy," Henry said softly.

Chris exploded. "Sure! *You* can say take it easy! *You've* got a shitload of scholarship offers! What about *me*?"

Henry's eyes grew so large that Chris knew his friend was as pained by the situation as he was. But the frustration was a cancer inside him. He sputtered with anger as he continued.

"All through school, I never made any grade lower than A. On anything! Shit, man, I'm goin' to be *valedictorian* of our class! I averaged seven-fifty on my college aptitudes! I scored ONE-FRIGGIN'-HUNDRED on my calculus placement! But just because my pa runs a dinky little feed store, they say we've got too much income for me to get financial aid from a decent school! What a joke! A little merchant like my pa hasn't got the six or seven grand a year it takes for tuition at a good college! Shit! I'm goin' to wind up at some state teachers college! Man, I'm never gonna get into a school with a first-rate biophysics department!"

Henry swallowed hard. "Slow down, Chris."

"Oh, Jesus! Slow down, he says! How can I slow down—when a dumb jock who doesn't know his anus from a terrene excavation gets the universe handed to him on a platinum platter!"

Chris was suddenly aware of his unwarranted personal attack on his friend. He fought to calm himself.

"Hey, Chris, I'm sorry, man." Henry groped for words. "But—It's not my fault. I—I just play basketball."

Chris forced a smile. "I know. I'm sorry too." Then his anger surfaced again. "Shit!" he barked. "Let's finish this algebra."

Henry bit his lip, looked away. Chris knew he had overstepped, that his friend was about to call it a night. Hoping to make peace, he went into an inspired imitation of Jerome Steele.

"Henryhenryhenry!" he bawled. "If you wanna learn this here algebra and pass that test tomorrow, you gotta work hard, stay sharp! You hear?"

Henry smiled. A moment later the two boys were back at work.

Whether Chris' hostility toward Jerome Steele was justified or not, one fact cannot be disputed.

From the moment Henry was thirteen and came under the tutelage of his junior-high-school basketball coach, Jerome was no longer able to contribute to his son's development as a ballplayer. From then on, the boy was under the aegis of professional mentors who taught the fine points of the game, fine points which Jerome did not know existed. Jerome's dog-eared, military-like basketball manual had done its job. Jerome had done his job. But now the pupil knew as much as the instructor—every word in the book. And more. Henry was becoming battle-tested. Jerome, so far as basketball was concerned, had never learned the lessons that combat teaches; he had never played the game. Henry rose now from the low plateau of Jerome's expertise to

52

rare heights which only his coaches and his own talent could navigate. Jerome remained below, looking upward and watching. He became nothing more than a cheerleader and moralizer, exhorting Henry, *ad nauseum*, to work hard, to stay sharp.

But Chris knew, even if Jerome did not, that Henry required no cheerleader. Drive, desire, determination— these qualities had been born in him. Often, when Henry practiced at night in the Elroy gym after dinner, Chris would sit in the stands and study. At those times, when only the hollow thump of the basketball echoed in the empty gym, Chris would marvel at the phenomenal concentration of his friend and reflect: What will power! And what Henry wills, Henry does.

Oddly enough, one of the reasons Chris most admired Henry was because of the loving way Henry protected Jerome.

Even after Henry became aware that his father knew nothing about the fine points of basketball, he would draw Jerome aside at team practices where everyone could see, and ask his advice. No matter how ridiculous that advice was, Henry would listen respectfully, nod in agreement, and seem to ponder as if the words had been sage. Then Henry would smile at his father and go out on the court and make miracles.

Thus are myths born, thought Chris, and legends embroidered. Because Henry loves his father and would never hurt or embarrass him, people are sure every move that fantastic friend of mine makes is because of that stupid old fart, old man Steele.

IV

In early spring of 1976, as Henry's magnificent senior year of basketball drew to a close, the recruiters increased their efforts.

There had been a flood of letters, offers from colleges in every state in the country. Now, the recruiters themselves descended on Henry—coaches, assistant coaches, alumni, preachers, senators, millionaires, famous athletes, movie stars.

They even used horses.

They flew him to Kentucky in a private plane. It was hush-hush, because the trip was against every recruiting rule in the book. But Jerome said yes, and Henry had begun to relish being courted by these famous and sophisticated men.

The private plane landed on a strip near Louisville. The wealthy Kentuckian who had accompanied Henry emerged first. Henry followed him down the ladder. Two other men were waiting.

"Henry, my boy. Good to see you. Good to see you," said the older of the two.

"Thanks," said Henry. "Same here."

"Welcome to the Blue Grass State," said the other man. He was tall, athletic, thirtyish.

Henry's eyes grew brighter with recognition. "Oh, my gosh, wow! You're—"

"Right."

"Hey, I saw every game you ever played on tv! I'm like your number one fan!"

"We know," said the Kentuckian who had brought Henry.

The tall man put his arm around Henry's shoulder. "Thank you for coming, Henry. I'm glad you decided to take a look at our campus. This is a wonderful place."

The group headed toward a nearby limousine. The older man said, "Our climate's nice. We've got lots of pretty girls."

"I loved going to school here, Henry," the tall man said. "Of course, I attended before Secretariat made Kentucky famous." They all laughed, and he added, "Would you like to meet Secretariat?"

"Yes, *sir*," said Henry. "I sure would."

"That can be arranged," smiled the tall man.

The Kentuckian who had accompanied Henry grinned, rubbed his hands together and said, "Yes, that can be arranged."

But mostly they lured with girls.

Henry stood on the topmost row of a Mississippi football stadium, looking away from the field at the panoramic view of the tree-filled campus below.

"If you come to our school, Henry, we won't recruit any other guards. We'll build our ball club around you. It'll be your show for four years, son."

"Yes, sir."

"Look down there on the football field."

Henry turned and looked down. On the field, spread from goal line to goal line, the college pep-squad drilled, charming in tight sweaters and mini-skirts.

"Ain't they nice, Henry?"

"Yes, sir."

"Which one d'you like?"

"Sir?"

"Come on, son. You know what I mean. Which one d'you like?"

"Oh. Uh, they all look alike from up here."

"Well then, Henry—let's just get ourselves a closer view."

The grinning men led him down the stadium steps toward the marching girls.

V

Two men entered the luxurious lobby of the Dallas hotel. One of them, a large, athletic type approaching middle age, quickened his step and strode directly toward the room clerk's counter. The other man—older, tall, thin, patrician—regally surveyed the lobby as he strolled toward the elevators.

An affluent-looking couple emerged from an elevator. The husband immediately recognized the stroller. "Coach Moreland Smith," he said.

With imperial calm, Moreland Smith bestowed his gaze upon the couple. His eyes were deepset, opaque, unyielding, ice-cold.

"I'm sorry to disturb you, sir," the husband stammered. "I'm president of a bank in California. Here on business. I, uh, I'm an admirer of yours. Just wanted to shake your hand."

"I thank you, sir." Smith's voice was crisp, but there was a trace of a midwestern accent.

"This is my wife."

Smith bowed, his smile radiating sudden warmth. The wife melted.

"So good to see you, madame," Smith said.

As the couple backed away, the big man who had entered the lobby with Smith came bustling toward him.

"Here's your room key, Coach."

"Very good, Phillips."

"Anything else I can do for you?"

"I think not."

57

An elevator opened its doors. Smith stepped in.

"Well, sir," said Phillips, "I think I'll have me a nightcap."

"As you wish. Good night, then."

"Yes, sir. Thank you, sir." As the elevator doors closed, Phillips added, "You really signed yourself up a good one tonight, Coach. Congratulations, sir."

The doors shut, and Smith's mouth formed a pleased smile that did not spread upward to his brooding eyes.

In his suite, he doffed his jacket and loosened his tie. For a moment he stood at the window, looking out at the skyline of Dallas thrusting heavenward in the near distance. Then he took a sleek, expensive tape recorder from his suitcase and set the gadget on the coffee table. He went to the bar, poured himself a tall Chivas, returned to the sofa and sat down. After a thoughtful moment, he snapped the tape recorder on to "record," took a sip of his drink and began to speak.

"Miss Rudolph, kindly transcribe this tape in its entirety."

He cleared his throat and took another sip of his drink. Then he rested his head against the back of the sofa, elevated his feet on the coffee table, closed his eyes, and spoke again.

"In your usual efficient manner, Miss Rudolph, please extract the salient points from what I'm about to say regarding Master Henry Steele and forward the information to the registrar's and athletic director's offices. Oh, yes, and to the attention of that Brunz fellow, the head of the Alumni Association. These offices will make all the necessary arrangements preparatory to Steele's matriculating at our noble institution of higher learning. Although these matters may seem routine, Miss Rudolph, this case presents a unique point or two.

"I have in my possession a letter-of-intent signed by our elusive young Hermes, I'm happy to say. It was an interesting chase and capture, and it stimulated me, Miss Rudolph. *Agnosco veteris vestigia flammae.* I feel again a spark of that ancient flame."

58

Smith smiled to himself, sipped again, and continued. "At any rate, we have him.

"Most of the material I'm about to dictate, Miss Rudolph, is background for my memoirs. Kindly destroy the tape when you have typed your transcription. Again, I importune you—and please forgive me for constantly doing so—to make absolutely certain no other eyes or ears see or hear this material. I have no wish, at this stage of my career, to expose my very rabid followers to the unwholesome machinations requisite to winning national basketball championships."

He sighed. "Well, on with it. June sixteen, nineteen seventy-six. Dallas, Texas."

Miss Rudolph's Transcript of Moreland Smith's Tape

During my odyssean endeavors as a college coach, I have recruited a panoply of the most gifted of American youth. From Lake Superior to the Rio Grande, from Montauk Point to Puget Sound, I have wooed wise-eyed urbanites with vowels on the ends of their names; thick-tongued southern blacks whose fourth-grade vocabularies are offset by magnificent basketball skills; bucolic midwesterners with giant bodies; street-wise ghetto savages with a highly creative approach to basketball. There are few surprises or delights I have not encountered in this duplicitous, intoxicating recruiting ritual. I have seen it all.

But I have not always been *the* Moreland Smith, creator of Western University's perennial champions, the most successful coach in college basketball history. No, indeed.

When I first began, thirty years ago, I bled in the pits of ambition with all the other assistant coaches. During my first ten years of coaching I was a nonentity, a desperate young man who scurried fifty thousand miles in some years by plane, train, bus, car—and, yes, by wagon, on horseback and afoot. Under the banner of whichever hicktown junior college or one-horse university was paying my inadequate wages, I cajoled, I flattered, I tricked young boys into joining my glorious cause. I have pandered, pimped, subverted and bribed.

I hated every minute of it. I loved every minute of it. Fiercely. As do all my coaching brethren. We are all collectively guilty. We are all collectively innocent. As lion kills to live, my confreres and I recruit in order to survive. Our employers demand that we hunt. If we do not, we starve, we die.

I have proved that I am the greatest hunter of them all. I am paid homage by awed parents and stuttering, obsequious high-school coaches. It has become an honor to play for Moreland Smith of Western University. And so I now personally recruit only the finest and most elusive prospects.

Henry Steele was a high-school junior when he was first approached on my behalf by one Armand Drake, a Western U. alumnus, a former California oilman who had relocated in the petroleum-rich Big Springs area of West Texas. Over a period of two years, Drake became friendly with the boy's father by purchasing two trucks from the gentleman. Drake was introduced to the lad, therefore, as a customer of his father's rather than as a representative of Western University.

I had read mountains of glowing press clippings, received constant and unabashedly laudatory letters from Western alums about young Henry Steele's achievements, watched whatever films I could get my hands on of Elroy High School basketball games. The films made my mouth water. All this, coupled with the knowledge that some of my most perspicacious coaching rivals were ardently courting the lad, made me determined to have Master Steele. So when Armand Drake finally called me and admitted defeat, saying that the boy was inscrutable and uncommunicative, I felt a heady call to combat.

I did what I seldom do these days. Drake sent his jet for me on the appointed day, and I spanned half a continent. The mountain came to Mohammad. I flew to Elroy last March—as you know, Miss Rudolph—to watch Henry Steele play ball. It was a most inconvenient time for me, in the middle of an undefeated season, but I was determined to induce that boy to spend his four years of college under me.

Between that night last March in Elroy and tonight here in Dallas, three months went by during which I could not obtain Henry Steele's signature on our letter-of-intent. Yes, I did make a modicum of progress. I found it encouraging when Steele refused to meet with me in Los Angeles, my home turf, and insisted on a neutral site such as Dallas or El Paso. I agreed, because during my single encounter with the youngster I had sensed an economy of mind which made him waste not. I deduced that the lad had already decided on Western, but that he wanted to bargain with me in a setting in which I would be as disoriented as he. I liked that.

We chose Dallas, and Armand Drake set the stage well, reserving a secluded corner of an elegant restaurant. My troops consisted of Phillips, my first assistant coach; Joey Wilson, the movie star, who is a nouveau nabob in the swarm of nabobs known as the Western University Alumni Association; and, finally, Terri Dymand. Miss Dymand is that sensual young creature who, in all her movies, disrobes at least twice. Drake and Wilson assured me that she would play a convincing scene with young Steele, both publicly and privately.

Drake arranged for his oil company's plane to fetch Steele. At Love Field, Drake met the aircraft and led Henry to the parking lot. There sat a gleaming, powerful new sports car, a . . . um . . . red Datsun 280Z, I believe. Drake handed Steele the keys and asked if he would care to drive the car to our restaurant meeting place. The boy merely shook his head no, handed the keys back to Drake, and got into the car on the

61

passenger's side. The incident made me recall my meeting with Steele last March in Elroy, when he hardly spoke to me, yet was vividly expressive with his silence.

The March night I speak of was the occasion of the district championship game. Henry's team had won, 94 to 49, and he had exhibited the most dazzling display of virtuosity I have ever viewed on a basketball court.

I left before the game ended. Drake drove me one block away to Steele's home where we parked and waited for the boy to come. I had no intention of waiting in line at the gym with my eager rivals, just one more face to be lost in the confusion. It was a risk, I admit, but I was prepared to lose him rather than queue up with the others. My image, you know.

At last Steele and another lad came walking toward us through the brisk spring night. Steele's posture, his unique, slouching athlete's walk was unmistakable, even from a block away. And his body language told me that he was down, unhappy perhaps; obviously, he hadn't accepted any offers at the gym that would make him run home, elated, to tell his parents. I got out of the car, instructing Drake to stay behind the driver's wheel. On the corner, under the streetlight in front of Steele's house, I waited.

Steele reached me and stopped. He said to his friend, "Night, Chris." Chris gave Steele a warm pop on the shoulder and went off.

"Hello, Henry," I said.

He smiled a respectful, civil smile.

"Do you know who I am, son?"

"Yes, sir." He said it as if he knew everything.

"Then you know, of course, why I'm here."

Silence. His silence said he knew why I was there.

"I trust that you resisted the blandishments my brethren undoubtedly proffered tonight at the gym."

"Yes, sir."

"You played a fine game tonight, Henry. I watched most of it."

"Yes, sir. I saw you."

62

Beautiful. Beautiful, Miss Rudolph. He not only scored over forty points, had more than two dozen assists and choreographed the entire contest, but this very cool young man had also counted the house. Suddenly I realized that Master Steele had executed a disproportionate number of his heroics immediately in front of where I sat. At that moment I knew I had him. I moved in, I attacked.

"Have you considered playing for me, son?"

"Yes, sir. I've thought about it."

He had *thought* about it. A fine little horsetrader. He did not imply *what* he thought about it.

An irritating thought jangled up from my subconscious. Looking into that boy's eyes, I saw my own eyes and realized—*this country boy is actually patronizing me!*

Very well. If he wanted to play on a national championship team, he knew how and where to find me.

"Well then, Steele, it has been good, indeed, talking to you. I happened to be in this area on other business and wanted to see, as long as I was here, if you were what they say you are."

He knew I was lying. He knew I knew he knew I was lying. He did not blink. Nor did I. We stared at each other. No other boy I have ever approached played mental defense like this lad.

"I really appreciate it, sir," he said and offered his hand.

I shook it and said, "Do you think it would be worth my while to pursue this matter further?"

"Yes, sir." Releasing my hand, he backed politely away a step. *He was actually dismissing me.*

"Mr. Drake will be in touch with you, son," I said.

As I got back into the car, Steele said, "Yes, sir."

That was three months ago. Tonight we had our second meeting in the restaurant.

An orchestra played sedate background music, but I could see the songs were not to Steele's taste. As the boy put away his *châteaubriand béarnaise,* he almost winced at the sentimental foolishness. Nevertheless, it was apparent that Steele was at ease in the expensive restaurant. His poise was commendable. The crystal chandeliers, the well-dressed clientele, the elegance of the place did not cow Master Henry Steele of Elroy, Texas. He has eaten many steaks in places such as this, I remember thinking at the time, and in company such as ours.

Phillips sat on one side of Henry, Drake on the other. I faced the boy across the table. Two empty seats awaited Joey Wilson and our nymphet. Steele had glanced at the empty seats, but evinced no further interest. We offered no explanations.

"How's the meat, Henry?" Phillips asked.

He spoke with food in his mouth. The man tends toward boorishness, Miss Rudolph, but that very quality makes him an admirable assistant coach. And though his obeisance to me is cloying at times, on the whole I find his servility an admirable trait, since his only function is to carry out my orders unquestioningly. I find it useful to have an acolyte like Phillips with me when I travel. He speaks to room clerks, taxi drivers and high-school coaches on my behalf. At receptions, he announces me to strangers. He disciplines athletes I deem in need of it. He does his job well.

"Bloody enough for ya, Henry?" Phillips persisted.

"Yes, sir."

"And the wine. Try it. It's excellent."

"Never mind the wine," I said. "Bad for the wind. Tell me, Henry, have you ever been to what is colloquially referred to as The Big Apple?"

"Sir?"

"New York City."

"Oh. No, sir. But I've heard a whole lot about it."

"Well, son, if you play for me at Western, you'll play at least once a year in the Garden."

"Chicago, too," Phillips blurted. "Chicago, Illinois. And Philadelphia, Pennsylvania, too. We go all over."

I silenced Phillips with a look, and then Drake chimed

64

in. "We're on national television more than any team anywhere, Henry."

"Yes, sir."

I felt it was time to drive for the basket, so to speak.

"Henry Steele," I said, "what can I do or say to induce you to play ball for me?"

He put his fork down, and very deliberately dabbed his mouth with his napkin. The boy was a joy to watch. No blushing. No stammering. No clearing the throat, no squirming, no hemming and hawing. No bravado. This young man is, as they say, "together."

Fortunately for the likes of me, however, lads like Henry Steele have no chance from the outset. You see, I had what Steele wanted. What chance does a callow youth, selling nothing but his body, have against successful, experienced, sophisticated men whose profession is the bedazzlement and subjugation of adolescents? Men such as I have pandered to the woefully predictable appetites of thousands of eighteen-year-olds. Our techniques have been honed and refined into an art.

Nevertheless, young Steele was a valiant battler, beautiful to behold.

After a moment, he spoke. "You have a good biophysics department." It was a statement, not a question.

"Yes, we do," I agreed. "Among the best in the world." I laughed. "Biophysics, eh? My young president of our university will be delighted. Here we have that rare combination—an athlete *and* a scholar."

"I'm not a scholar, sir," Steele said drily. "My buddy is. He's a big brain. His name's Christopher Blair."

I acted surprised in order to maintain my bargaining position with the lad, all the while recalling how many times in the past I had given two scholarships—the extra one usually being for a teammate, or a brother, or a girlfriend. What touched me in this case was that Henry's motive seemed to be born of a sense of justice and merit, rather than friendship alone.

"You're asking for an athletic scholarship for yourself *and* an academic scholarship for your friend?"

65

"Yes, sir." He leaned forward and said, "Each scholarship is for four years. No-cut. With everything. Books. Tuition. You know what I mean, sir. Everything."

Drake said, "Henry, I don't think you realize—"

"Yes, he does." I couldn't help chuckling before I repeated, "He does."

Henry sat back, and our eyes met and locked. I smiled first, smug in the knowledge that as soon as Henry thought he had won, *I* had won. He smiled back at me.

I could not resist saying, "A philosopher named Santayana once wrote, 'What sometimes looks like American greediness is merely love of achievement.' "

He digested my words, then said, "Yes, sir."

"Well, Henry—" I began.

A stir in the restaurant heralded the arrival of my un-needed reinforcements. Joey Wilson and Terri Dymand swept through the dining room. Heads turned as other diners recognized the two beautiful, stardust-spreading, larger-than-life people. We all stood to greet the newcomers.

"Joey, my lad," I said. "Henry Steele, meet Joey Wilson, the actor."

Before Henry could answer, Joey put an arm around his shoulder and said, "Hello, everybody. Good to meet you, Henry."

"Wow!" Henry seemed suddenly quite young. Wide-eyed. It is, as I said, Miss Rudolph, an uneven war. "I've seen all your movies," Henry stammered.

Joey grinned. "Meet Terri Dymand. Terri, say hello to Henry Steele."

Though Terri worked like Marilyn Monroe, the lad, to my surprise, seemed to regain his composure. His countenance hardened momentarily and then he smiled and returned Terri's gaze in the manner of—excuse me, Miss Rudolph, but the appropriate word must be used—in the manner of an experienced cocksman evaluating his next piece. I sighed to myself. Too bad. I

66

wanted Steele to be young in all ways. But I knew that Terri was no novelty to him; he had had many Terris.

Joey said to Terri, "Do you feel like dancing?"

"Yes, I do," she breathed. Turning again to Henry, she pouted her lips into an open kiss. "Shall we?"

"I don't dance very well," he said. He was looking not at Terri, but at me. There was business to be concluded.

"I'll teach you," Terri exhaled.

His eyes met mine. I almost laughed in his face despite the fact that I loved his stubbornness.

I winked at him and spoke. "I don't think there's anything more to say, Henry. Your terms are acceptable." I shook his hand. "I'm gratified you've chosen Western University, son. Welcome."

His eyes reflected every candle in the room. His smile was a delight. I like the boy, Miss Rudolph. One minute he's like a cynical old emperor, the next minute he's open, childlike.

The last I saw of Henry and Terri, they were leaving the restaurant together about an hour ago. Right now, they're probably in one of the rooms here in this hotel, Miss Rudolph, doing it for dear old Western.

VI

A July morning, early, not much past seven. The sacks of cottonseed pellets, cattle feed that farmers and ranchers scatter over grazing land, had arrived the previous night and been shunted to the rail siding behind Chris' father's feed store. Shirtless, Chris walked into the freight car, hoisted a bag to his shoulder and carried it, slightly rubber-legged under the weight, across a wooden dock and into a storeroom, where he placed it gently atop a growing stack. He had been at it since dawn. Chris had always aided his pa whenever he could. Much of his studying had been done either behind the store counter or at the desk in the tiny office at the rear of the store.

These days, however, Chris was using the labor as therapy to allay his anger and self-pity. Henry had said nothing to him about the "deal" with Moreland Smith. (A true conservative by nature, Henry had considered the possibility that the deal might fall through; he had decided to wait for confirmation of the agreement with Smith.) Meanwhile, Chris suffered. He had been accepted by the West Central Texas Industrial and Agricultural College of Rocky Arroyo, a town sixty miles from Elroy. The tuition at WCT I&A was $127.50 a semester for state residents. Chris would live at home and commute daily in his mother's '61 Valiant. He had quipped to Henry: "At the end of four years, I'll probably be qualified to teach high-school chem in a place like Elroy."

Now, perspiration made Chris' torso and face glisten. On his way back to the railroad car, he paused to survey his work. He had hardly made a dent in the load of feed—only the area near the door was cleared. He leaned against the door jamb to rest, toweling himself with his bandana.

"You just get out of the shower, Chrissie?"

He whirled. Henry lolled against the dock wall, smiling a peculiar smile.

"How long you been there watchin' me, man?" Chris said.

"Most folks take their showers at home, Chris. Didn't you know that?"

Chris laughed. "What are you doin' down here so early?"

"I came over to ask you somethin'. That letter of acceptance. From West Central Texas I&A?"

"Yeah?"

"You got it here?"

"Sure. It's in my pa's desk."

"Can I see it?"

"Sure. How come?"

"I wanna compare it to a letter I just got."

"Oh. Sure. I'll get it."

They went into the small office. Chris took the letter from a drawer in the ancient rolltop desk and handed it over.

Henry read the letter, emitting occasional "ahs" and "ums." His face was quite serious. When he had finished, he looked up at Chris and then deliberately ripped the letter into shreds.

"Hey!" Chris squealed. "What the hell's got into you?"

"The letter is unsatisfactory."

"I know it! But it's the best I got! Best I *had*."

Henry dropped the shreds into the wastepaper basket and smiled. "It ain't the best you got."

With a huge grin, he produced another letter from his

pocket and thrust it toward his befuddled friend. "This is better!"

"What is it?"

"Read. Read."

Chris read. The missive was from the Registrar of Western University. It was addressed to Christopher Blair, care of Henry Steele.

Dear Mr. Blair,

We are happy to inform you that after reviewing the excellent transcripts of your grades forwarded to this office from the Elroy, Texas, High School at the request of Dr. Moreland Smith of the Western University Department of Physical Education, you are hereby extended a four-year scholarship, renewable semi-annually on the basis of your academic standing at the end of each semester. Please advise this office promptly if . . .

Henry and Chris celebrated.

The red 280Z sports car had arrived that morning at the Steele home. With it came an envelope bearing the return address of Mr. Armand Drake of Big Spring, Texas. The envelope, addressed to Jerome, contained a bill of sale for the car, a registration certificate, and an insurance policy. Now, as Henry guided the red car over dirt ranch roads in excess of sixty miles an hour, both boys were smashed on Lone Star Beer. They had killed two six-packs before Henry put his first fifty miles on the odometer.

Like a vermilion rocket, the car left a billowing trail of umber dust that exploded from the back tires and hung in the hot West Texas air. The boys whooped, hollered, yelled. They laughed so hard they could not see. They sang. Chris played Beethoven on his harmonica. Once, when Henry crossed a low gulley at high speed, Chris almost swallowed the harmonica. The boys thought that very funny. Soon afterward, they both got out of the car and vomited. They thought that was very funny, too.

They shot through herds of cattle, scattering terrified beasts in their dusty wake. As Henry took a curve near the blacktop on two wheels, he and Chris waved happily to a parked patrol car. The two deputy sheriffs in it chuckled. One of them said, "Sure hope he don't blow a tube. Then we'll have to ship him to Western University in a box." They watched Henry speed out of sight at eighty miles an hour.

At last, where a dirt road petered into empty desert, Henry parked the car near a butte that cast a bit of shade. Chris checked the area for rattlers, then sat down in the shade and opened another can of suds. Henry stood before him, raised his can of beer and proposed a toast. Henry had great difficulty standing; Chris had great difficulty focusing on his friend.

"Lazies and genitalmuns," Henry said. "This is the first time I broke trainin' since I was three days ol'!"

"I'll drink to tha'," Chris mumbled.

They drank.

"Hey, wait! I forgot!"

"What'd you forget, Henry?"

"I broke trainin' with Terri."

Chris, looking up at his friend, thought: He grins like a vampire when he's drunk.

Henry continued. "All night, one night. In a hotel. In Dallas, Tezus. Ohhhmmmman, that Terri Dyman'!"

" 'Ray for Terri Dyman'!"

"And I broke trainin' with 'nother girl in Miss'ippi."

" 'Ray for tha' girl, too!"

"And a girl in K'tucky. And Waco. And Tuscaloosa. And, uh, lotsa places."

" 'Ray for alla them!"

"But—I never drank beer b'fore." Drained, Henry plopped down on the shady ground.

Suddenly, Chris began to sob. "Henry, Henry," he wept, "I really thank you, Henry, for gettin' me a scholarship to West'n University."

71

"You're welcome, Chris. Only, you don't gotta cry. Okay?"

"I really mean it! I couldn't get a decent school! West'n's got a great biophysics department! Number one!"

"An' a great basketball team, too. Also number one. But, hey, Chrissie, you don't gotta cry."

"But I'm so *happy!* Man, Henry! Two full scholarships *and* a car!"

Henry began to cry too.

In a moment they ceased their weeping. Before them, despite its coat of West Texas dust, the red car gleamed in the relentless afternoon sun.

"Henry, ain't it 'gainst the rules for a college to give a car?"

Henry laughed. "Yeah."

"How'd they do it?"

"Easy. The guy Drake, set it up so's it looks like my *Dad* gave it to me. For a graduation present."

"Slick," Chris said. A new thought crossed his mind. He giggled. "Hey, I hear those California chicks're somethin' else, eh, Henry?"

"Chicks are chicks. They *use* ya, man," Henry said. He smirked. "So *I* use 'em right back."

"You shouldn't feel that way." Chris began to cry again.

"Gimme 'nother beer, willya, Chris?"

"Sure, Henry."

"And come on, man, you don't gotta cry." Henry jumped to his feet and gave a magnificent bloodcurdling, rebel yell. "Ah-oooooooo-eeeeee!" he screamed. "California!"

Chris managed to stand. He, too, wailed, "California!"

Together, they bayed to the West Texas sun above them, "California! CALIFORNIA!"

VII

Between the time Jerome went bankrupt and Henry reached the age of thirteen, the Steeles did not own a car. Jerome had walked the half-mile to and from work each day. The focal points in Eunice's life—grocery, variety and dry goods stores, meat market, roadside fruit and vegetable stand, library, church, doctor's office—were all within a three-block radius of her house. Henry's school was across the park, less than two hundred yards from their front door.

The day Henry's junior-high basketball team was to play its first road game, forty miles away, Jerome bought a car, a nine-year-old '64 Plymouth, for $75.

To Jerome and Henry, the car's only function was to get them to and from road games. For Eunice, however, the '64 Plymouth was a temple of salvation. As her life increasingly whirled around her son's growing fame; as she heard children whisper in the grocery, "That's Henry's ma"; as her friends opened conversations with, "My husband says your boy sure did Elroy proud in that game last night"; as men of stature in the community—the mayor, the sheriff, Reverend Wells—crossed rooms to say hello to her and Jerome; as she shared this glory and smiled and, despite herself, took pride in their newly achieved place of honor—as all this happened, Henry Steele's mother knew she was only a hasty word, an accidental moment away from losing control of herself. She loved her son, was awed by the miracle of his athletic abilities. But when he came home from school at

73

five, gulped dinner, went back to the gym till nine, returned home and, without studying, went to bed, she hated Jerome for having twisted her baby into an intense, silent, blank-faced automaton. She would feel the lump in her throat thicken, and knew it was a dam holding back her insanity, that one day the dam would give way and her craziness would inundate their lives. So she measured everything she did and said when she was in company. Often during the day, as she cooked and cleaned, she talked to herself. Entire afternoons went by when the tears did not leave her eyes. When neighbors popped in through the open back door and saw her red eyes, she told them she had just chopped onions. After one such incident, she locked the back door and pulled the shades and kept them that way. The house became her prison. Until Jerome bought the car.

Reverend Wells was a dry, comfortable old man, a father to his flock. Eunice found temoprary respite in his church, but no lasting peace.

Often, when a visiting evangelist was allowed to preach, Eunice felt herself about to give way to the frenzy in the church. The more fervently her fellow congregants went to their knees and screamed their hallelujahs, the more will power it took to repress the tumult inside her. She trembled, bit her lips, dug her fingernails into the palms of her hands, clutched her Bible. She desired release, but dared not indulge herself. She was not like the others, she felt, for if she once let go, she would never be the same again. They'll take me off to the crazy house, she thought.

One Sunday afternoon, two years before Henry was graduated from senior high school, as a visiting evangelist ranted, Eunice fled from the church. Outside, she stood in the bright afternoon sun for a moment, her eyes searching the ghostly main street emptied by the Sabbath, the deserted park across the highway, the barren plain beyond that. Across the park, she saw Jerome and Henry walk toward the gym and enter it. Eunice's gaze

74

swept back to their house, a block away. There, in the rear driveway, sat the '64 Plymouth.

Blinded by tears, she walked to the car. The keys were in it. Jesus had left them there for a purpose. She would kill herself.

Moments later the car was on the open road outside the Elroy city limits, climbing toward ninety miles an hour, screaming toward nowhere.

At a fork in the highway, Eunice angled off the blacktop and roared along a gravel road for several miles. Then she left the gravel with a skidding, two-wheeled slide that straightened onto a rutted dirt road. In the distance, to her right, she saw a huge boulder, large as a house, in the middle of a cactus field.

She wrenched the wheel toward the boulder, and the car, lurching, left the road. Her foot went all the way down on the accelerator. Above the roar of the motor, Eunice screamed, "I'm comin', Papa! I'm comin', Mama! I'm comin'! Oh, God! Jesus Christ, help me!"

A hundred yards from the boulder, the old Plymouth ran out of gas. It bucked twice, shuddered, ran partway up a sandy dune, coughed and stopped.

Eunice sat there, uncomprehending. Then her eyes sought the instrument panel, realized that the needle was on Empty. She turned off the ignition key, rested both arms on the steering wheel and cradled her head on them.

In a moment she began to sob, sob as she had never sobbed before, great animal wails that spent themselves only after half an hour had passed.

The sun was setting behind the boulder when she was able to open and focus her eyes. On the car floor below her lay her Bible, open. She glanced at the page and read: "The voice of one crying in the wilderness, Prepare ye the way of the Lord, make His paths straight."

She lifted her head. Beyond the boulder, sunset painted the sky flamingo. The rays were almost parallel to the plains around her. Every rock looked like a diamond. The coral sand stretched toward the horizon, touched the sky in a spectrum of violet. Eunice got slowly out of the car and looked around. It was the first time she had noticed color in years. She walked to the boulder, kissed it. Pressing her lips to its flinty surface, she saw every tiny grain of its composition. From far away the rock had looked dark brown; now she saw rivers of color, patterns of reds and purples and ochres, sunbursts of beauty. She laughed.

From somewhere beihnd her, she heard a motor. She looked. A dustball grew. A rancher's panel truck materialized, pulled up to her.

"Evenin', Mrs. Steele," the ranch-hand said. "Can I be of service to ya?"

"Good evenin'. I came out here to read my Bible . . . the sunset's so beautiful, don't you think? I . . . uh . . . I seem to've run out of gas."

"Don't you worry none. Ranch pump's a few miles yonderway. Just wait here, and I'll be right back."

By the time Jerome and Henry came home from the gym, Eunice had made a salad and the hamburger patties were ready to throw on the oven broiler.

"You men hungry?" she sang out.

They halted and stared at her. She was smiling. "Somethin' wrong?" Jerome said.

"Not a thing in the world!" Almost shyly, she went to Henry, stood on tiptoe and kissed his cheek. Pleased, the boy put his arm around her and returned the kiss. "Just glad to see you, that's all," she said.

On her way back to the oven, she lightly touched Jerome's elbow and smiled at him again.

"We're glad to see you, too, Ma," said Henry. He looked at his father.

"Oh, yeah. Me, too," barked Jerome.

At dinner, Henry said, "You go to church this afternoon, Ma?"

"Yes, I did."

"How was it?" Jerome asked.

"It was just fine," Eunice said.

Next day she left the back door unlocked and raised the window shades. She sought out her neighbors and chatted with them. All the days that followed, while Henry practiced in the gym and Jerome sold used cars, she read her Bible. She became the second most active member, after the Mrs. Reverend Wells, in the church's ladies' auxiliary.

At basketball games, with Jerome squirming, exulting, suffering, shouting, cheering beside her, she smiled benignly. At night she slept well. She did not abandon her campaign to persuade Henry to pay more attention to his friends and to study his books more, but now she fought without rancor. For the axis of her universe had tilted. She was able to accept the loss of her son because she had gained Jesus Christ.

The owners of ranches around Elroy and the county law officers all knew that once or twice a week Eunice Steele drove out of town, found a place to park in the wilderness and read her Bible. What they did not know was that, as she sat in her car amid pristine beauty, she also studied God's canvases, and, like Michelangelo, reproduced them in vivid colors on the chapel ceiling of her mind.

VIII

That summer, as Henry prepared to leave for college, Jerome presided over a tranquil domicile. During Henry's adolescence, Jerome's bristling defensiveness had slowly changed into a rough amiability. Although he still barked when he spoke, he was civil to Eunice, a civility that at times even bordered on kindness.

The night before Henry was to leave for California, however, Jerome prowled the house like a man who knew he would be facing a firing squad at dawn. Thunderclouds piled high on his brow; his bark was louder than usual. Eunice knew that Henry's leaving meant an unfillable void in her husband's life. On the basis of Jerome's past behavior in times of travail, she prepared for disaster.

Henry's idea of packing consisted of taking a garment from his bureau drawer and, with a one-handed push shot, tossing it across the room and into the open suitcase on his bed. Entering the room, Eunice caught a pair of wadded-up pajamas as they flew toward the valise.

"Hey, nice catch, Ma."

"Let me pack for you, darlin'," she said. "You hand me whatever you want to take, and I'll fold it and put it in the bag."

"Thanks."

Jerome came into the room carrying a cardboard carton full of trophies. "Don't forget these," he barked.

"Dad," Henry said gently, "I don't want to take any trophies with me."

"You take 'em. Most of 'em are still in the livin' room, but you take these I picked out. To remind you of how hard you worked to get 'em!"

Henry and Eunice smiled. "Yes, sir," the boy said.

"Too bad Chris isn't drivin' to California with you, sweetheart," Eunice said.

"He wants to stay and help his pa until the last minute," Henry told her. "This is their busy season. And Coach Smith told me to report early."

Eunice folded a shirt. "Henry, Coach Smith promised us you wouldn't have any trouble with your grades. How can he make a promise like that?"

"He can make a promise like that," Jerome shot at her, "because coaches like Smith take care o' basketball players like Henry. Right, Henry."

"Right, Dad."

Softly, Eunice said, "I thought Henry was goin' to college, not basketball camp. Gettin' an education is why a person goes to college."

Jerome's laugh was a mocking bray. "Gettin' a pro contract is why *Henry's* goin' to college. Right, son?"

"Right."

Eunice was determined to have her say. Addressing Jerome, but looking at Henry, she said, "I just thought that since Henry hardly opened a book all the way through high school, he just might have to pay more attention in order to—"

"To learn about the matin' dance of the tsetse fly?" Jerome barked. "Who cares about all that, Eunice? What's in them books is donkey droppin's! What a man *does*, that's what they pay off on in this here life! Right, son?"

"Right, Dad."

Dawn, cool and clear. The September sun waited just below the horizon. Only the chirps of desert birds perched on phone wires interrupted the morning quiet.

79

In the Steele's backyard, Jerome and Eunice watched as Henry, wearing his letter jacket, doublechecked to make sure that everything had been loaded into the small red car. Satisfied, he closed the hatchback door with a soft thump. Frightened, the birds flew from the phone wires with a sudden fluttering of wings. Father, mother and son stood looking at each other.

There was nothing now to say or do. Everything had already been said. Everything had already been done. They had spent their lives up to this moment talking and doing. Henry had been born in this house, grown up in it. He had been suckled by this woman, walked in the security of this man's visions for as long as he could remember. He knew their weaknesses, their strengths. He knew they loved him. He loved them.

The boy went to his mother. They hugged. For a moment, as she pressed her head into her son's shoulder, she wanted to say: You'll come home again sometimes, won't you, Henry? I feel like this is the last time we'll ever see you here, in this town, in this backyard. You'll come home again? But she said nothing. Her arms released him.

The low car was between Jerome and his son. Standing by the open driver's door, Jerome tried to smile but managed only a benevolent grimace. Henry walked around the car, ready to embrace his father. But before he could raise his arms, Jerome stuck out his hand. They shook hands, a long, hard squeeze, their eyes locked. Jerome was the first to ease his grip. He stepped back, touching his forehead in a half-salute. Henry smiled and watched his father walk clear of the car. The goodbyes were over.

Almost. As Henry got into the car, he paused to stare at the old backboard and basket over the garage door. Then he slammed the car door shut, threw a final wave at Eunice, and started the motor. He shot backwards out of the driveway. On the street, before he shifted into first, he looked at the two people standing in the yard. They waved.

The car roared away. In a few seconds, Henry was out of his parents' sight. The last faint sounds of the car's motor faded into the stillness of the dawn.

Eunice went into the house. In the living room, she sat down in her rocker, holding her opened Bible in her lap, and stared out of the window.

When Jerome came in from the yard, she pretended to read. She was afraid to confront him, terrified that he would fall apart as he had once done eighteen years earlier.

Jerome crossed to the fireplace and took the Winchester down from its mounts on the wall. He found a box of shells, put it in his shirt pocket, cradled the rifle and went to the door.

"J'rome?" said Eunice, horrified.

"Yeah?" His voice was subdued, lifeless.

"What on earth are you fixin' to do?"

He actually smiled, but there was no animation in his face. He said, "I got me some linseed oil down at the car lot. This here thing ain't been cleaned for a while. I'm goin' huntin' in a few days."

"That's nice," she told him inanely.

"Yeah. Mayor and sheriff and Reverend Wells. They been askin' me for years. Figure I'll take 'em up on it this time."

"I'll see if your huntin' clothes need any fixin'."

"Thank you."

"You're welcome."

"Uh . . ."

"What, J'rome?" Nervously, she closed the Bible.

"Uh . . . don't worry about me. I'm gonna be all right this time. I . . . uh . . . can handle it."

She managed to smile at him.

He said, "Be bad for Henry if anythin' happened to me. He'd worry. Take his mind off o' what he's got to do. Can't let that happen. He's got to stay sharp."

"I see."

"That's all I care about."

81

"Henry."

"Henry. So don't worry about me. I plan to keep myself busy." He meant to laugh, but it came out a snort as he said, "I might even join the church again."

He walked out, closing the front door firmly behind him.

Eunice tried not to think about Jerome. She tried not to think about Henry. She opened her Bible.

BOOK TWO

I

Twenty years earlier, as an office manager in a large Manhattan corporation, she had discovered that a memo signed by B.J. Rudolph had more clout than one signed by Beatrice Jayne Rudolph. By the time competing males in remote departments of the company learned that the twenty-five-year-old B.J. was a woman, she was a minor executive, entrenched in the corporate structure.

Five years later, however, she languished in the same job, with no promotion in sight. At the same time, her marriage disintegrated. B.J. found herself roused by a young man who worked in her office, went to his apartment and stayed the night. Forthrightly, she confessed to her husband and asked his forgiveness. He sued for divorce. She did not contest the suit.

B.J. withdrew her last few thousand from the bank and caught a plane for home, a small town in Indiana. After a period of no more occupation than being babied by her parents, she took a job with a local junior college, just to have something to do. The junior college assigned her to the athletic department. One of her many bosses was the basketball coach, a tall, aristocratic, middle-aged man named Moreland Smith. This was his first season as head coach.

Two years later, Smith's team was ranked number one among the nation's junior colleges. He became the most important man in that small part of Indiana. All his requests were promptly complied with. One request was that B.J. Rudolph work only for him, at a nice increase in pay.

The next year, when Smith left to become head basketball coach of an ivied New England college, B.J. went with him. Smith and she were a team. Her good judgment, her efficiency and loyalty, combined with his tactical brilliance and ability to handle boys made them a formidable machine, geared for winning basketball games. Publicity, budgets, tickets, schedules, transportation, intra-faculty dealings, gym maintenance—she told him each morning how she planned to handle each problem; he nodded approvingly; she disappeared and left him free to view game films, diddle with X's and O's and dream of new strategies for the next foe.

Western University had lured him from New England in 1964. B.J. went with him.

Though she was now forty-five, her sex life was flowering. She loved very young men, the smoothness of their faces, the hardness of their bodies. She wanted no entanglements or protracted affairs, only release. These man-children had what she desired, and she took it—easily. Her figure was classic, seductive and firm. Her face, always handsome, and now further beautified by a face lift during a Brazilian vacation, was alive with intelligence and humor. Every young Adonis ached for her. She accommodated a goodly number of them.

In Moreland Smith's office, B.J. gave him a stack of papers to sign. Waiting, she sat on the window ledge and surveyed the campus below.

The athletic department occupied the top floor of the phys.-ed complex, an H-shaped cluster of buildings. Western University's magnificent gym was one leg of the H. The other leg consisted of intramural gyms; olympic swimming pool and stadium; handball courts; weightlifting, wrestling and boxing rooms. The connecting part of the H was a three-story building—classrooms on the first two floors, varsity athletic offices on the third.

Directly below the window of Moreland Smith's office were two square blocks of tennis courts, their artificial surfaces evergreen in the bright California afternoon. Beyond and on both sides of the tennis courts lay huge intramural playing fields surrounded by running tracks complete with sawdust pits for long-jumping and pole vaulting. The H-shaped phys.-ed buildings, the courts and the fields filled almost a square mile of the heart of the immense Western University campus.

Even from a distance, B.J. spotted Henry Steele. It was not merely his green-and-white jacket and his burden of two suitcases and a dufflebag that held her attention; it was that the boy's innate dignity was not hidden by these awkward burdens or by his weariness. When he drew closer and stopped, overwhelmed suddenly by the sight of the tremendous gym, B.J. caught her breath.

The sun glinted off Henry's brown hair, giving it red highlights. B.J. speculated that his eyes were blue, his skin smooth, his body hard. From his jacket, she deduced that he was a jock. She hoped he was a basketball player.

Moments later, glancing through the open door of her own office, adjacent to Moreland Smith's, she saw Henry appear at the top of the stairs that opened in the center of a student's lounge. He looked around, spotted the "Athletic Department" sign on the door of her suite, and came forward, suitcases dragging. He entered the suite at top speed and did not slow down until he had burst into Smith's office. The coach, his back to the door, stood studying his playbook.

"Hi, Coach Smith."

The coach turned, annoyed. "Young man, can't you see I'm busy!"

By now B.J. had caught up to Henry. "May I help you?" she asked gently.

Henry did not know whom to address. He stammered at Smith, "You said that—" then turned to B.J. "He said that I should see him as soon as I got to Los Angeles."

87

"Who are you?" barked the coach.

The boy's eyes widened. He swallowed. B.J. thought tears would come any moment.

"I'm Henry Steele." It was a whisper.

Like an electric light snapping on, a smile warmed Smith's face. "Henry!" the coach said. "I'm sorry, son. I've seen so many boys the last few days. Welcome."

The coach proffered his hand. Henry shook it. His relief and happiness exhibited themselves in a deep, breathy laugh.

But Smith's mind had already gone back to the charts on his desk. Politely, he asked Henry, "How do you like L.A.?"

"It sure is, uh, different, sir."

"Yes. Well," Smith said, "Miss Rudolph will take care of you. It's good to have you with us, Henry."

"Thank you, sir."

"This way, Henry," B.J. cooed. Smiling but firm, she led him out.

In her own office, she appraised Henry at close range as she went to a file cabinet. "Your last name is Steele?"

"Yes, ma'am."

She found his card and walked briskly to her desk, where she picked up a notebook and several envelopes. "This is your playbook, Henry. Bring it to practice Monday. This is the phone number of your tutor, Janet Hays. Get in touch with her before next Friday. You're to see a Mr. Gonzales about a job. He'll be on the football field at eight-thirty every morning. Sooner you see him, the better. Here's a catalogue and enrollment material. This is alumni association material. Your alumni Big Brother is Mr. Howard Brunz. *He'll* get in touch with *you*. Here, in these envelopes, are two tickets to every home game. And here—"

"Excuse me, ma'am," interrupted Henry. "I prob'ly won't be needin' any tickets. I don't know anybody to give 'em to."

She supressed a smile. "They're for Mr. Brunz."

"Ma'am?" He stared at the envelopes. "I don't understand."

"You will." She winked at him.

She handed him the rest of the envelopes in such rapid succession that he was hard put to find a place for them. When his pockets were full, he held envelopes under both arms and one under his chin. Enjoying herself thoroughly, B.J. put the last envelope in his mouth. He clenched it between his teeth.

"You're assigned to number three dorm, room twenty-six," B.J. said. "Now you're all fixed up. Any questions?"

"No, ma'am," Henry said. "I guess not."

He picked up his suitcases, and B.J. strapped the dufflebag over his shoulder.

"Where's dorm three?" he asked.

"Out the front door of the building, turn left, go two hundred yards, and there it is. Don't worry, we wouldn't let you sleep more than two football fields away from the gym."

Biting her lip to keep from laughing, she followed Henry out of her office, through the foyer and to the door leading out of the athletic department. Here, after making sure no one was looking, she grabbed one of his buttocks and gave it a friendly squeeze.

Startled, Henry looked back over his shoulder at her.

"Elevator's over there," B.J. murmured. " 'Bye." She went back to her office humming.

On the main floor of the athletic building, Henry stopped to stare at the trophy cases that lined the walls. Then, dragging his baggage, he moved slowly from case to case, reading the inscriptions on the cups, plaques, statuettes and citations in the glass-covered displays. At the end of the hall he came to a ramp with a sign above it: "To Gym Floor."

Despite his weariness, Henry's eyes lit up. Slowly, he walked the length of the ramp until he reached the semi-darkness of the gym floor. For a moment, until his eyes adjusted to the gloom, he saw only a yawning blackness. And then, slowly, a miracle took shape.

A vast hardwood floor, gleaming even in his unlit space. Mountain-sides of seats, looming upward on all sides of the playing floor, disappearing finally into the ceiling far above. My God, Henry thought, I can't even see the roof!

On the wall near him, he spotted a panel of switches. Tentatively, he snapped one on.

High above him, a single bank of lights shone. Henry caught his breath, awed by the half-lit splendor of the gym. Then he snapped on another switch, and another, and another, until all the lights blazed down. A hundred suns! His eyes swept the arena, end to end, floor to ceiling. Ah! Tucked high against the ceiling, a half-block up in the air, were eight glass backboards and baskets, held by long metal legs attached to the roof.

Henry looked again at the panel of switches. Did he dare? With a little smile of anticipation, he snapped on the entire bottom row of switches. A low buzz. A bump! The legs were moving! The backboards, like giant spiders descending in their webs, were lowering on their metal legs!

Henry felt organ music thunder inside him, a majestic Bach-like diapason. Holding his breath, he moved out on the gym floor, spinning, turning, gazing up at the oncoming baskets. His eyes burned; he blinked now in order to see. At center court, he stopped, marveling in disbelief at the expense of hardwood that swept away on all sides. Eight baskets! Four separate courts—three crossways, the main court longways!

The music swelled inside him. A lump formed in his throat. His heart pounded; his body ached. Never, in his entire existence, had he been so happy! For eighteen years he had lived and worked—why? For this. For this. He was home!

The big man was munching an apple when he came

into Room 26, Dorm 3 and found Henry Steele slumped over a desk in deep sleep.

The big man finished his apple and flipped the core into a metal wastebasket, but Henry ignored the dull *bong* sound. Taking a package of Fritos from the top of the desk, the big man ripped it open. At the crackling of the waxed paper, Henry opened his eyes, though his head still rested on the desktop.

His eyes focused first on a pair of enormous shoes, then moved slowly upward. The shoes were attached to two equally massive legs. The massive legs were topped by great, muscular thighs that almost burst through the jeans that encased them. Above the thighs, a narrow waist widened suddenly into a herculean chest. On top of the chest were ponderous shoulders and a neck so thick with muscle that it seemed wider than the head above it. The head's face, grinning, peered down. The lower jaw moved up and down, up and down, pulverizing mouthfuls of Fritos. A hand brought another load of Fritos from the bag to the mouth.

"Hi," the big man said.

"God!" was all Henry could answer.

"No, I'm not God. I'm Tom."

Henry sat up. The room spun for a second.

"Hi. I'm Henry."

Rising, he extended his right hand, and Tom's huge paw gave him a helping pull upward in mid-shake, until he was steady on his feet. He saw now that Tom was about six-foot-six, six inches taller than he was.

Henry rubbed his eyes and yawned. "I went to Coach Smith's office and a lady told me to come here. I hope there hasn't been a foul-up."

"If that's what the lady said, then I guess we're roommates." Tom crumpled the empty Frito bag and shot it into the wastebasket. "You can have that side of the room."

"Thanks."

Fighting the stiffness in his back and legs, Henry moved his luggage across the room. The room was

L-shaped. At the base of the L was the entrance, two desks, a small icebox and sink. The narrow top of the L held two beds, each parallel to the wall and separated by a narrow walkway leading to a window.

"You want to go get something to eat?" asked Tom. "Let's go get a hamburger."

In a booth at the Burger King, they demolished sandwiches and malts.

"They got Burger King in Texas?" Tom queried.

"Oh, sure," Henry said. "We got all the fine restaurants. Burger King. MacDonald's. Wetsons. Jack-in-the-Box."

Tom stared, then decided that Henry's statement stemmed from true innocence. He grinned.

Henry went on. "Of course, all we got in Elroy is the Elroy Cafe. Nice place. Pecan pie's super. But all the others—MacDonald's and all—they're all within fifty miles of home. That's nothin' in Texas. And if we want seafood, they even got a Fish Palace in Bloodshot Junction. That's seventy miles away, but worth it. Super catfish."

"Sounds great."

They smiled at each other, and then Tom laughed. "So you ran into the horny nympho?"

"The what?"

"Coach Smith's secretary. B.J. Rudolph, the red-nosed nympho. That's what we call her."

Henry was fascinated. "How come?"

"Last season she got hold of our star center right before a big game. He played thirty minutes and scored two points. I never saw a guy play so lousy and be so happy."

Captivated by the anecdote, Henry forgot to chew for a moment. "How long you been on the team?" he said at last.

"This is my second year on the varsity. You know, it's a good sign for you—that they stuck you with me. As

92

my roommate. Usually they don't put a freshman with a varsity guy. You must be pretty good."

"Oh, I'm okay." Henry was quite matter-of-fact about his own basketball skills. Without bravado, he merely stated his belief in himself.

"They get you a job yet?" Tom asked.

"I think so. You got a job?"

"Shit, I go to this old fart's house who went to school here in 1932. Or maybe it's 1832. Anyway, he gives me five bucks an hour to wash his cars. Last week I spent four hours on one door handle."

Henry laughed, impressed. "Hey, I hope I get a job like that!"

Tom finished off his burger. "You make All-American and they'll make you the crocodile exterminator. Twenty bucks an hour for keeping crocodiles out of the gym."

Eyes widening, Henry asked, "There's crocodiles in Los Angeles?"

Tom almost choked on his last bite. "Hell, no, Henry!" He swallowed. "Hey, think I'll have another burger. You want another one?"

"No, thanks."

"Gotta build up my strength, so I can make a dynamite impression on Coach Smith at our first practice session."

Henry pondered this statement briefly. Then he said, "Maybe I'll have some fries."

Smiling, Tom led his new roommate back to the counter for additional sustenance.

II

Dear Dad and Mom,

I've heard Rev. Wells talk about PARADISE before. Well, paradise can't be any better than my first two weeks in college. But classes haven't started yet. They start Monday. I hope I still love it then, ha ha. (Don't worry, Mom. That's a joke.) Also hope, Dad, I don't get any mumbly professors. Only professor I met so far was over the phone—my tutor, Miss Hays. She talked right out, really clear.

I got a job helping take care of the grass on the football field and will probably earn over $200 a month. Pretty good, huh?

My roommate Tom (I told you about him on the phone two weeks ago) is really a nice guy. We don't see each other much because he's an upperclassman and it takes them a whole week to pick courses and get enrolled. But when basketball practice starts, Tom and me will go together everyday.

Mom, I had some dates with a pretty girl. Her name is Julie. She's a sorority girl. I met her at a banquet for freshman athletes. She has a big car and we drive around some. Her father owns a factory.

Dad, this campus is really something. I spent a whole afternoon at the football stadium. Wow! Seats over 75,000. I watched the football guys work out. Some of them live in my dorm. I also visited some men who are important in my career. The basketball team's trainer is a really nice old guy. His office is bigger than the whole locker room and showers in Elroy gym put together. He spent a whole hour showing me how to bandage my ankles. I visited Coach Phillips, too. He's Coach Smith's top assistant. Coach Phillips is from the South, and he's a lot like you, Dad.

Mom, the food here is super. The training table is like a great big cafe, right in the basement of my dorm. My room is way up on the third floor. I've got a mailbox in the lobby all my own, so write me, please.

Haven't seen Chris yet. I'll look him up next week, after classes start and I'm really settled.

Dad, I'm working hard on my game. Every morning I go to the gym and shoot around until lunch. In the afternoons I run track and use some of the great muscle machines they have for improving your legs. I get into pick-up games, too, to stay sharp. Then at night after dinner I go back and shoot around some more by myself at the gym.

Well, as Bugs Bunny says, th-th-that's all f-f-folks. Or was it Porky Pig?

Your joking son,

Love,
Henry

Henry's euphoria was indeed genuine. He was with his own kind, young men whose concerns and goals, conversations and interests, coincided with his own. He had described this world as paradise, and he meant it. Henry was truly home.

Nonetheless, three small disturbances had tainted those first weeks slightly, had left him confused for a moment or two.

He had spotted Gonzales as soon as he walked out on the playing field of the mammoth, empty football

95

stadium. The chunky Chicano was guiding a mower over the grass carpet, leaving a swath of green velvet behind him.

Henry trotted over. "Mister Gonzales?"

Gonzales slowed the mower, then cut the motor. "I'm Gonzales," he said. He spoke with an accent.

"Hi. I'm Henry Steele."

They shook hands. "*Buenos dias*, Henry Steele."

"I'm supposed to see you."

"Sure. Here I am. What about?" Gold teeth flashed as the man grinned.

"About a job," said Henry.

The grin vanished. Suddenly cold, Gonzales snapped, "Okay. This way."

Henry followed him across the field to a metal box set into the base of the grandstand.

Pointing to the box, Gonzales said disgustedly, "The sprinklers go on at six and off at eight."

"Yes, sir. Uh, night or morning?"

"*Hijo de la*—! Night!" Gonzales glared. "Your pay is four bucks an hour. I wish *I* played goddam football."

"I play basketball."

"Football, basketball, you're all the same to me. A bunch of freeloaders! Hell, I'm paying one three-hundred-pound yerk five bucks an hour *to watch the grass grow*! When it gets two inches high, he *tells* me, so *I* can mow it. That's the only yob he can handle. Hell, *el burro sabe mas que el*! Big dope!"

Fuming, Gonzales walked away.

"Sir?" called Henry.

"What?"

"Uh, where do I pick up my paycheck?"

"*Hijo de puta!* You haven't even worked yet, and you want to get paid! Why don't them coaches cut the crap and yust give you guys the money straight out, instead of sending you over here to bug me!"

"Well, I—I just—"

Gonzales waved his arms. "You pick up your paycheck Fridays at Miss Rudolph's desk."

"Yes, sir. Thanks."

"Now leave me alone, man. I got work to do."

As Gonzales went back toward his mower on the opposite sideline, Henry heard him mutter, "Next thing they gonna pay 'em for taking a chit!"

Henry headed for the exit, noticing as he crossed the field that all around him small, copper-colored sprinkler heads were rising from the grass. And then suddenly the sprinklers had been turned on. Water sprayed all over the huge field. Within seconds, Henry was soaked.

Frantic, he shouted toward Gonzales. "I didn't do anything! I didn't touch that box! Honest! I didn't turn the sprinklers on!"

Laughing, Gonzales shouted back, "Are you kidding, man? You couldn't turn 'em on if you wanted to. They automatic! They turn on by themselves." He was still laughing as he started the big mower, and then the machine's thunder drowned out his mirth.

Confused, Henry sprinted fifty yards through the watery spray to the exit.

The second small disturbance of those first weeks had occurred when he called his tutor, the day after his meeting with Gonzales.

From his room, Henry dialed the number B.J. Rudolph had given him. He sat at his desk, holding the phone receiver between his shoulder and cheek, and picked up a basketball from the floor. Listening to the number ring, he spun the ball, Harlem Globetrotter style, on the end of his index finger.

Finally, a young woman's voice said crisply, "Hello."

"Is, uh, Janet Hays there?"

"This is Janet Hays. Who's calling?"

"My name's Henry Steele. I'm callin' about gettin' tutored."

"Fine. What's your classification?"

"Oh, I'm just a freshman." He made the spinning ball travel down his finger, over the back of his wrist and up his arm to his elbow, where he flipped it into the air and caught the still-spinning ball again on his index finger.

"I see." Janet's manner was businesslike. "Then there are a couple of things we'd better get straight. You come to *my* apartment at *my* convenience. And you only stay *one* hour. I'm pretty booked up, and I've got my own studies to think about, too."

"Sure," said Henry. He transferred the whirling ball from the index finger of his right hand to the index finger of his left hand. "Um, when should I come?"

"When you have a problem." Janet laughed. "My Lord, classes haven't even started yet."

"Oh. Uh, when do classes start?"

Again she laughed, a warm, rich sound. "I don't believe this! Didn't you pay attention when you went to freshman orientation?"

Henry knit his eyebrows together for a moment. "What's *that*?"

When she spoke again, he sensed the change immediately. The warmth was gone; her voice was cold, flat.

"You're a jock, aren't you?"

Henry stopped spinning the ball and held it in his lap. "Yes, ma'am. And they told me—"

"—to report to the coach," she interrupted. As if talking to an imbecile, she said, "But they didn't mention anything about enrollment or what subjects you're taking."

"Right," Henry said.

He thought: Two in two days. First Gonzales, and now this tutor, both jock-haters. Wow! He had never before encountered anyone who disliked athletes.

Janet's words came quickly, as if she wanted to get the conversation over with. "Well, I'm not a damned freshman counselor. Get the coach's office to pick your courses and get you registered. *Then* call me. Get a pencil."

Frantically, Henry searched the clutter on the desk until he found a pencil.

"I live at four-six-one-five East Wood Way, Apartment seven, second floor."

"Just a minute, please." Henry could find no paper. "Would you mind sayin' your address again?"

She repeated it, slowly intoning each word, then spelling it, as if she were instructing a fool. Henry inscribed the address on the handiest available surface—his basketball.

When it was done, he said, "Thanks. You know, I'm really goin' to need your help. When it comes to books, I'm not too smart."

"No shit," she said and hung up.

He stared at the dead receiver for a moment, then shook his head. "Holy crud," he whispered.

The third disturbing incident of those early weeks happened that same night. This incident, however, produced only faint unease.

Only an hour after Henry spoke to Janet Hays, B.J. Rudolph solved his registration problem, simply by sending one of her assistants, a graduate student in the school of educational administration, to register for him. Then, when he asked how to go about getting Chris' phone number and address, she took his hand, led him to her office and dialed the registrar. While she was getting the information, she did things to Henry's hand that made his jeans seem terribly tight in the crotch.

Unannounced, Henry went to Chris' lodgings, an ancient rooming house in a neighborhood packed with rooming houses.

The front door was open. In the living room, students lounged on old sofas and armchairs. Most of them wore jeans, sandals, beads. Henry asked for Chris and was directed to the topmost floor.

He climbed the three flights, repelled by cooking odors and by the dank smell of unwashed clothes and bodies. Chris was not in his room.

Through the open door, Henry surveyed the tiny cell.

99

The ceiling was too low to stand up straight anywhere but in the center of the room. There was barely enough space for the cot and tiny desk. For a bookshelf, Chris had stacked reinforced cardboard boxes, which were filled with his texts and papers.

Gloomily, Henry went back downstairs, where a young man with hair halfway down to his waist said that Chris might be at the meeting over at Indie Hall.

"Where's that?" Henry asked.

Through thinly veiled contempt, the hirsute student told him where Indie Hall was located. Henry was glad to leave. These dreamy-eyed, overly-relaxed aliens with beards made him uncomfortable. He did not know why.

At Indie Hall, a large wooden building that had once been a church, some kind of rally was going on. Students of both sexes milled about on the front lawn, fiddling with signs that proclaimed Cesar Chavez this, and Cesar Chavez that.

Henry entered the auditorium. On the stage a speaker harangued the packed house. Henry's quick eyes found Chris near the back of the room, his arm around a girl's shoulder. She was attractive, but a little plump, and she wore an Indian band and a red feather in her long, loose hair. Both the girl and Chris seemed absorbed in the speaker's words, but occasionally, during the audience's cheers and shouts of agreement, they kissed.

Disoriented and confused, Henry wheeled and walked swiftly out into the clean night air. At his dorm he picked up his workout gear, then went to the gym and sought refuge on the basketball court. That night he practiced for almost three hours.

Aside from the small discomforts caused by Janet Hays, Chris and Gonzales, those first weeks were as Henry had written his parents—paradise. He had especially enjoyed the banquet for freshman athletes, held his second day on campus.

The banquet hall, a ballroom high in the student center, reflected the importance of athletics at Western

100

University. The room glittered with silver, crystal, flowers and white cloths on long tables. Behind the speakers' table, a massive sign read, "WELCOME WESTERN U. FRESHMAN ATHLETES." At the head table were coaches, Moreland Smith among them, and athletic department officials, university administrators and alumni. These elders glowed benignly at the young men at the lesser tables. The boys themselves all wore badges proclaiming their respective games and names. Henry's said, "Henry Steele is my name; Basketball is my game."

As the boys ate, nubile sorority girls served plates of cookies and pitchers of milk. Regular waiters moved about doing the real work.

The mountainous tackle to Henry's left looked over and said, "Hey, Tiny Tim, ain't you gonna finish your eggs?" Without waiting for an answer, he took Henry's plate, put it on top of his own empty one and dug in. "Pass them rolls thisaway," he said.

The basket of rolls was twelve feet away to Henry's right, where sat Wheeler, a seven-foot-tall basketball center.

"I'll get 'em," Wheeler volunteered. Standing, he tilted his huge body toward the rolls, stretched his right arm to its limit and easily palmed the distant basket. He handed the basket to the tackle, who dumped its entire contents into his plate.

A dapper man in his sixties, sporting a sand-colored regimental mustache, rose and clinked a spoon against a glass for attention. The room fell silent.

"My name is Howard Brunz," the man's deep voice intoned, "and I'm the new president of the alumni association. Before our first speaker addresses you, let me introduce our lovely hostesses and the houses from which they come." In turn, he presented each sorority girl. The last to be named, and by far the most dazzling, was one named Julie, who stood near Henry. As she took her bow, she smiled directly at him. Henry returned the smile.

101

She was stunning—a Norse goddess with silver-blonde hair in a silken waterfall to her waist.

She came down the table toward Henry, bestowing milk and cookies. When at last she stood directly behind him and leaned forward to fill his glass, her breast touched his ear. He heard her heartbeat, smelled her gardenia perfume. His whole body tingled.

As Julie moved away, she dropped a small piece of paper in his lap. Henry read the note. It said, "JULIE— 475-5099—Tri-Gam House." She was already a few yards away, but she was watching him. He grinned at her and she nodded with her eyes.

The principal speaker at the banquet was Simon Bell, Western University's athletic director. Henry agreed with every word he said.

"I welcome you freshman athletes! *You* are the *chosen few*. The Western University varsity athletic program is THE HOME OF CHAMPIONS. And *you* have been chosen because we believe that you men have the ability and *desire* to be *winners*!

"Yes, WINNERS!

"Now, certain people say WINNING is a dirty word. To them I say this: high-school and college athletics are the last bastions of self-discipline and devotion to duty left in America! If folks like *us* don't *stand strong*, our nation will succumb to the forces of weakness and subversion.

"*So, for the sake of our great nation*, we must *pledge ourselves* to WINNING!

"I'd like to recite a poem written by a poet—and a *man*—Brother Howard Brunz, president of our great Alumni Club.

"Heed these words, young warriors,
Ere your struggles begin;
Winners never quit,
And quitters never win.

"Heed these words, young warriors,
For soon the battle ensues;
And my lads, it's not how you play the game,
But *whether you win or lose!*"

After the banquet, Simon Bell stood at the ballroom door so that he could shake each athlete by the hand as he departed. Moreland Smith came up behind Henry at the door.

"This is Henry Steele, our little oil well from Texas, Brother Bell," announced the basketball coach.

"Oh, yes?" Bell looked Henry up and down. "Kind of small, isn't he, Brother Smith?"

Smith put his arm around Henry's shoulder, an uncharacteristic gesture of affection. "Yes, sir, Brother Bell, he's kind of small." The coach emphasized each of his words knowingly. "*And—kind—of—fast!* This young gazelle here is going to out-quick a lot of very surprised folks. If I may paraphrase Samuel when he spoke of Jonathan and Saul, Henry is swifter than eagles, stronger than lions."

Bell beamed. "Well, well! Splendid! I'm looking forward to seeing you in action, Henry!"

Henry was in hog heaven. "Thanks a lot, coach! Thanks a whole lot. Thanks, Mister Bell!" He shook their hands and backed out of the room, still gushing. "I really mean it! Thanks! Thanks a whole lot. 'Bye, Coach Smith, Mister Bell. I really do like it here!"

III

He rang the bell at the door of Janet Hays' apartment and waited. When no one came right away, he looked into the peephole on the door. The peephole opened, and he found himself staring into a lovely green eye. Embarrassed, he stepped back.

Janet opened the door a crack.

"Hi," he said. "I'm Henry Steele."

She opened the door wider, and his smile of greeting froze in astonishment. Another green eye, as lovely as the first. A strong straight nose. Cupid's bow lips. A perfect, rounded chin. Reddish-gold, shoulder-length hair.

Henry's gaze took in the rest of her. Her full, firm breasts were in no way diminished by the overly large sweatshirt she wore, and her legs, in tight, faded jeans, were shapely.

Janet had also looked him over. She laughed. "You're pretty puny for a jock."

He winced.

"Come on in." She stood aside so he could enter.

In the apartment, he saw a man sitting on the unmade bed. The man was about thirty, bearded, barefoot. His shirt was unbuttoned. He sat absorbed in the book on his lap and did not look up.

Janet closed the door, bustled into the kitchen alcove and began rinsing some dishes. "I'll be with you in a minute," she called.

"Can I sit down?" Henry asked.

Janet stopped her dishwashing. Half contemptuously, half teasingly, she addressed the other man. "Malcolm, what do you think? *Can* Henry sit down?"

Henry flushed, but saw that Malcolm was paying no heed to Janet's hazing.

"If your legs bend the right way, Henry, then yes, you *may* sit down. Over there." Janet indicated a chair at the dinette table in the center of the large, one-room apartment. "That's your first lesson in English." Sensing that Henry was debating whether to stay or not, she smiled. "I'll be through in a minute, Henry."

Henry sat, books on his lap, and waited. After a few moments, Malcolm glanced up, searched the table with his eyes, reached for the notebook he sought.

"You gettin' tutored, too?" Henry asked.

Malcolm gave him a glare of contempt, then returned to his book. Henry was insulted by the rebuff. Janet, being a girl, could get away with murder, he thought, but not this snooty cow-chip.

Finished with the dishes, Janet went to a desk behind Henry, sat down and quickly typed a few sentences. Then she handed the typed page to Malcolm, who perused it and nodded approval.

"That's better," Malcolm said. "Depersonalization manifests itself in nonpathological, partially adaptive situations of realistic external stress."

Henry stared.

"Yes!" exclaimed Janet. "I see! And depersonalization is only *one* example of a regressive ego state?"

"Correct," said Malcolm.

"Oh, Malcolm, thank you so much. If it weren't for you—"

"—you'd do just as well, Janet my love." Completing the sentence for her, he puckered for a kiss.

"You're sweet." Janet was about to oblige when she remembered Henry's presence. She touched her finger to her lips, then to Malcolm's in a proxy kiss. Embarrassed, Henry looked away.

105

Malcolm stood and buttoned his shirt. "Have you seen my shoes?" he asked Janet.

"They're right there," volunteered Henry. "Under the, uh, bed."

Malcolm slid his feet into the clogs, gathered his books and moved toward the door.

"Oh, I forgot," said Janet. "Malcolm, Henry. Henry, this is Malcolm. I'm his T.A."

"Oh," Henry said. "Congratulations."

Janet laughed. "T.A. stands for Teaching Assistant, dummy. Malcolm's an instructor in the psych department. I work for him."

"Oh."

Arm in arm, Janet and Malcolm went to the door. Henry heard them kiss, heard Malcolm say, "Janet, my love, call me anytime," heard the door close.

Janet came back to the table, sat down and smiled at him civilly. "Sorry you had to wait. Your hour starts now. Okay?"

"Sure," said Henry. Placing his books on the table, he sat at attention, ready to be tutored. He saw she was looking at the typed sheet she had shown Malcolm.

"What are you workin' on there?" he asked.

"Term paper. For a senior psych course." She put the paper aside.

"Oh. And, uh, that fella—he helps you out with it?"

She laughed, a superior laugh. "Henry, *I* ask the questions. I'm the tu*tor*. You're merely the tu*tee*." She assumed a businesslike air. "What courses are you taking?"

Henry began searching through his texts and notebooks for his list of courses. All his texts, brand new, crackled when he opened them. In his looseleaf, packages of dividers and notebook paper were still wrapped. A small carton of unsharpened pencils fell from the notebook. Smiling shyly at Janet, he picked them up, explaining, "School supplies." He put the pencils in a plastic pencil case fitted into his notebook. Entertained, Janet waited patiently.

106

At last he found his list of courses. As he read each one off, she wrote it down on a notepad.

"English IA," he read. "History IA. Introduction to Social Studies. Synergistic Techniques in Prepubescent Kinetic Development."

Her pencil stopped. "What's that? Synergistic Techniques in—what? What's the subject matter?"

"How to coach peewee basketball," he replied earnestly.

"Heavy." Janet laughed and put her notepad aside. "Let's start with English. Do you have an assignment sheet?"

He found his English textbook, shook a mimeographed sheet from inside its cover and handed it to her.

"Ummm, by tomorrow," Janet said, reading, "you're supposed to be up to page one-hundred-ten in your text and halfway through Moby Dick. All right, tell me—what problems, specifically, are you having?"

Henry grinned. "I don't know yet."

"Have you read up to page one-ten?"

"No."

"Have you read up to page *ten*?"

He gave an embarrassed shrug. "No."

She stared at him. "Then perhaps *I* can tell *you* what the problem is. You never learned to read."

If she were a man, Henry thought, she would now have a cracked jaw.

Janet sighed, rose, and put his opened text before him. "Just start studying. When you come to something you don't understand, ask me."

For a second, she had an impulse to apologize for insulting him. But four semesters of tutoring jocks compelled her otherwise. Flippantly, she said, "This is study period, not play period. And, um, that high-school color-jacket. Do you have to wear it indoors on a warm day like this? I've heard of security blankets for infants, but really, Henry—a big boy like you? The world won't stop turning if you take that jacket off."

She went to the desk behind him and began to type.

107

He sat frozen, furious. Should he walk out? If he did, would the coach be angry? Or would they get him another tutor, one who would understand what his priorities were and why he had come to Western U.?

Janet stopped typing and crossed the room in search of a book. As she leaned across the bed to take it from a shelf, Henry was treated to a sensational view of her behind, shapely in the tight jeans.

She straightened, turned, and saw his steady eyes on her.

"What are you looking at!" Angrily, she hit the book with her open palm. "Shit! You think because the athletic department gives me two-fifty an hour to tutor you animals, you can sit there studying my ass? Forget it! You've got no chance with me, Jack!"

They glared at each other. Henry's impulse was to grab her and shake her until she screamed, until her superiority disintegrated into fear. But though he knew he could not match words or wits with her, he tried.

"I'm not an animal!" he snarled. "And I wasn't studyin' your——. Look, I didn't do nothin' to you. I just came here to learn!"

She laughed cruelly. "I've never met a jock yet who had brains enough to learn anything beyond the coach's playbook and junior-high-school sex."

Suddenly the anger left her face. Touching the open textbook on the table before him, she said simply, "Read."

She went back to her desk and resumed typing.

Henry sat immobile for a moment. I hate that stuck-up bitch, he thought. I'll show her! Goddammit-to-hell, I'll show her!

His eyes focused on the page before him. His body tensed. As if it were an enemy, he attacked the text.

An hour later, when Janet announced, "Time's up," he rose, gathered his books and left with only a nod.

She called after him, "See you next week, Henry," in a tone that was both friendly and patronizing. She had used that tone many times in the past after being forced to put a jock-stud in his place before she could continue as his tutor. It had always worked. Questioning the jock's intellect, usually on valid grounds, effectively castrated him. Then she could earn her two-fifty an hour in peace. She needed the money badly. She was only a junior now and she planned on a doctorate, which would take another several years after she graduated.

From her doorway, she watched Henry walk stiffly down the stairs and out of sight. Well, she thought, no more trouble from him. She smiled to herself. Too bad; he was kind of cute.

IV

At the cafeteria, he asked for Chris.

"You Henry?" the manager asked.

"Yes, sir."

"Chris told me all about you. Great kid. Best dish-washer I ever had. I been here twelve years, and Chris is the only washer I ever had who can keep up during the dinner rush hour." The manager pointed. "You just go right through those big doors and on into the kitchen back there. You'll see him."

"Thanks."

In the kitchen, Henry watched his friend wield a soapy sponge in a sinkful of dirty dishes. No hands ever washed dishes with more joy and energy.

Chris' hair, only medium long back home in Elroy, now covered his ears and the top of his shirt collar, and the stubble of a mustache dirtied his sweaty upper lip. His white uniform was limp with the perspiration brought on by the enthusiastic tempo of his dishwashing.

After a moment, Henry moved closer. "Hey, Chrissie," he said gently.

Chris' smile was born of honest pleasure. "Henry! Oh, man, it's good to see ya!"

"How ya doin'?"

"Swimmin'ly." Chris made swimming motions with his hands in the sink. "Get it? Swimmin'ly?"

"I got it. Now, how do we get rid of it?" Henry was only half joking as he stared at the sink full of dirty dishes.

"Get rid of it? I don't *want* to get rid of it. I *love* it, man!"

"This?"

"Everything, Henry! My job! School! California!" Chris grinned. "California *women*!"

"That's great, Chris." Frowning, Henry went on. "I been tryin' to get over and see you, but seems like——"

"Hey, just stop, okay? I know you're busy as hell. I can dig it, man. I can dig it."

"How come you're talkin' like that?" Henry said sharply. " 'I can dig it.' You sound like a cruddy hippie."

Chris only grinned.

Henry continued his assault. "And how come you're growin' a mustache? You need a shave, Chrissie. And how come you're letting your hair grow so long? Your folks know you're growin' long hair?"

Chris began scrubbing dishes again. "My life's changed, man," he said soberly. "Naw, my folks don't know about my hair or mustache or the way I talk. You see, Henry—my folks're back home. And I'm here. On my own. Free."

Henry frowned again. "You like where you're livin'? If you don't—I mean, I ain't seen it—but if you don't, I can help you get somethin' else."

"Henry, I live in a really neat house. Man, everybody is everybody's friend. Hey, let's talk about you. How's basketball?"

Henry ignored the question. Motioning toward the sink, he asked, "How much they pay you to do that?"

"Buck and a quarter an hour." Chris smiled. "Thanks to you, man, that's all I need. Food and clothes money. And I eat here a lot for free. Scholarship pays for everything else. Hey, how's your job?"

"It's okay."

Henry studied the perspiration on Chris' face.

The doors to the kitchen opened and a student waitress carrying a stack of pamphlets approached them. She was pretty—appealing, sexy.

111

"Hi, Christopher!" the girl said. "Here're the flyers. Hand them out tomorrow morning between classes in front of the library."

"Gotcha, beautiful," beamed Chris. "Ain't she purty, Henry?" To the girl he said, "Hey, my hands are wet, honey bunch. Would you put 'em over there?"

"Anything you say!" The girl kissed Chris on his wet cheek, more than just a sisterly smack, put the pamphlets on the counter and left.

"I'm handin' those flyers out for a guy who's runnin' for congress," Chris explained. "He said some things that kind of switched me on."

"Man, you're into everything."

"*Damn* right!" Chris bubbled. "Hey, you know what? You ought to come with me to the next meetin' of—"

"No thanks," Henry interrupted. "You know I don't go in for that—stuff." He had almost said "shit."

"Yeah," Chris sighed. "You just play basketball."

They looked at each other.

"That's right, I just play basketball," Henry said.

They were silent for a moment, and then they turned away from each other. Henry was the first to speak.

"Chris, I, uh, gotta get back to my, uh, job."

Chris' grin was tinged with sadness. "See you around."

"Yeah. See you around."

Henry headed for the football field. In another hour the sprinklers would turn themselves off and his toil for the day would be done.

In the kitchen, Chris plunged happily back to his dishwashing. In another hour he would be finished here. Then a couple of hours of studying, a rap session, a meeting, a little love-making, a little more studying, a little more love-making, a little more studying. . . .

Chris began to sing as he worked.

V

In his early years at Western, Moreland Smith discovered that one of the perils connected with winning national titles was the constant loss of assistant coaches. Other colleges would hire them away, reasoning that an assistant to a perennial coach-of-the-year like Smith would know the master's secrets; or, better still, might even be an integral factor in the master's winning formula. The reasoning was false, but the steady departure of assistants was nevertheless a nuisance. Smith thought about the problem and came up with a solution. He found a man who had no virtues whatsoever that would motivate another college to steal him. He found Phillips.

Phillips had no concept of basketball strategy, no imagination, no ability to project beyond that day's workout and Smith's standing orders. Phillips had no leadership qualities that did not stem from brute power; the boys obeyed him because he relayed Smith's orders. His cloddishness was a known fact everywhere. At parties there was always a drift away from wherever he happened to be; his idea of humor was a full-throated series of racial and outhouse stories from the hill country. He was a woman-chaser. Somewhere off-campus, Phillips had a wife and children, but he was often seen around the university with adolescent females of the big-breasted, dimwitted variety.

Because of the man's virtues, however, Smith ignored his crudeness. He was a drill-sergeant extraordinaire, a single-minded, narrow-minded, tough-minded philistine of unquestioning loyalty.

Six years earlier, Phillips had been coach of a junior college team in the hills of eastern Tennessee. A scout had reported to Moreland Smith, verbatim, Phillips' first speech of the year to his newly gathered players: "Awright, you turkey turds, I don't believe in pep talks. I teach basketball, not bullshit. Don't fuck with me. I'm tougher'n any of you. So make sure your asses are wound up tight durin' practice, else I'll be handin' you your lazy balls for dinner. Cocksuckers who won't put out in practice lay down like yella fairies durin' games. On my team, you're gonna *hustle* and *go*, you sumbitches, ev'ry minute."

With one exception, Smith agreed with the essence of Phillips' reported oration, although his own expression of the same thoughts was infinitely more eloquent. And therein lay the exception. Smith *did* believe in a certain amount of what Phillips called bullshit—Virgil, Shakespeare, Donne, the Scriptures, Santayana.

The first team meeting of the season was held in early October in a small classroom across the hall from the gym. Henry and his teammates listened in awe as Smith, standing on the elevated lecturer's platform, concluded his greetings.

"Gentlemen," Smith said, "excellence is not achieved through talent alone. Excellence requires *Resolution*! *Desire*!

"And, as Shakespeare said, 'Let not the native hue of your resolution be sickled o'er by the pale cast of excessive thought.' In other words, gentlemen, when you're told to do something, *don't think about it*. Just *DO* it! The moment you're told to do it. This club is not a democracy. We don't debate about or vote on *anything*."

Smith impaled the boys with his gaze.

"This year, here at Western, I am giving you the opportunity to do what is almost unique in college basket-

114

ball annals. You have the ability, the talent, to go through this season—*undefeated*. But, do you have the desire? Do you have the mental toughness and intestinal fortitude to make the supreme sacrifice? To ignore all else in your lives—family, girlfriends, weaknesses of the spirit and flesh—and dedicate yourselves to the task at hand? If you do not, I don't want you here! Get out! Now! There is the door! Go back to the slums and ghettos and hicktowns that spawned you. Go back to mediocrity and the company of ordinary men.

"But if you have dreams, and if you are men enough to make them come true—*this is your chance for greatness*! Go and catch a falling star! Make your dreams come true! You can do it! You can do it!"

Finished with his speech, Smith stood before the squad, a messiah staring at the back wall of the room, seeing into worlds they could soon enter if they only dared. His words echoed in Henry's head, seared themselves on his mind.

Phillips rose suddenly from his seat in the first row and growled at the squad, "All right, you turkies, let's GO!"

A deep-throated rumble, like the beginning of a mastiff's growl, emanated from the boys and rose to become a bloodcurdling roar. The room exploded into activity. Shouting, "All *right*! Let's go! Let's get 'em! What'd'ya say! Let's *go*! Let's *GO*!" Henry and his teammates stormed from the room toward the gym.

There were about twenty men on the varsity squad. With the exception of Henry and three other freshmen, all the players had been on the previous year's national championship squad. Despite their seasoning, however, all the returning men—including one All-American and two all-conference selections—knew that they would have to battle for a starting position.

In the gym, the squad ran several laps in single file, clapping their hands and shouting encouragement to themselves.

115

Smith nodded, and Phillips' whistle shrilled. "Guards line up here," he shouted. "Forwards and centers over yonder."

Eight guards, including Henry, lined up shoulder to shoulder. Smith, a general inspecting his troops, walked along the line.

"I want this man's legs built up," he said to Phillips, who took notes on the clipboard. "Put this man on a weight-lifting program. This fellow's got a belly since last spring; see that he loses it."

In the presence of the full squad, Henry was painfully aware that he looked like a midget in the company of giants. At five-foot eleven, he was five inches shorter than the next smallest player.

As the coaches moved away, he realized that Tom was standing next to him. "Hey, man," Henry said under his breath. "What are you doin' in this line? Don't tell me you're a guard!"

"Yeah, I'm a guard." Tom grinned down at him.

"A six-six guard? Hell, where I come from, some teams don't have centers as big as you."

Tom laughed. "I was the smallest man on my high-school team. Tallest was seven-four."

Henry forced himself to look at the guard to his right, a black player named Floyd. Floyd was as tall as Tom.

God! thought Henry. He swallowed hard. For the first time, doubt grabbed his innards.

Supervised by Phillips, the squad labored for two weeks under a harsh regimen of exercises and drills designed not only to get the boys into top condition—thereby saving them from the agonies of pulled hamstrings and charley-horses—but also to cull those boys too weak-hearted to endure the endless hours of pulling, lifting, propelling, pressing, shoving and forcing an army of muscle-building machines.

Henry did well those first two weeks. Spirited, determined, speedy, fantastically well-coordinated, he drew pleased grunts from Phillips and, from his command

116

post on the catwalk that circled the practice gym, More-land Smith smiled his approval. On press day, Smith put his confidence in Henry on record for the whole sports world.

The reporters, each with a press kit that included a bio and an in-action photo of each player, gathered before the squad. They took notes as Smith introduced each man. Pencils flew. Camera bulbs flashed.

The coach had been typically reserved when he introduced each boy, especially the stand-outs from the previous year's team. He had learned long ago that college boys were often harmed by too-lavish public praise. But when Smith came to Henry, he put his arm around the boy's shoulder and beamed.

"And here, gentlemen," he told the reporters, "is someone you'll be hearing a lot about. To paraphrase Edmund Spenser, 'He blesseth us with his two happy hands.' This young man is a fine ballhandler, among other things. Meet Henry Steele of Elroy, Texas."

The reporters found Henry's photo and bio in their press kits. Photographers maneuvered for a good picture-taking angle.

"You'd better get a good look at him right now while he's standing still," Smith purred, "because when he gets going, he's nothing but a blur. Off the record, gentlemen, we're expecting big things of Henry."

Flashbulbs popped. Posing, grinning from ear to ear, warmed by the patriarchal weight of Smith's arm on his shoulder, Henry was truly in paradise.

VI

By mid-October, the squad had been cut to fourteen men; the frills, the exercises, the calisthenics had become secondary to the actual playing of basketball itself. Now Moreland Smith came down from his catwalk and took a close-up role in the practice sessions. From the very first one, Henry's paradise began to change inexorably into hell.

It began well enough.

For almost an hour, Smith stood in foul territory just behind the basket and watched as Phillips fed each boy, in turn, a bounce pass from the baseline. When the boy received the ball, he would execute whatever maneuver Smith had called for. Stop, jump and shoot. Or, drive for a lay-up. Or, pass off to the man behind you.

By the end of that first hour, Smith and Phillips took Henry's effortless skills for granted. Although the other players, all amazingly talented, equaled Henry's performance most of the time, none matched his clean, machine-like precision. Henry's shots went in every time, almost always without touching the rim. The other players slam-dunked so hard that the backboard shook and the rim quivered for half a minute afterward, or they flew through the air like huge birds to put in reverse lay-ups and other breathtaking shots. Henry took nervous note of his teammates' skills; they were doing things with a basketball he had never seen before outside a televised pro game. Characteristically, he became even more like an automaton. Fake. Dribble. Jump. Shoot. No matter how upset, he could maneuver under the basket in his sleep. But inwardly, Henry trembled.

Phillips' whistle blew. "Okay, you peckerwoods," he barked, "now we're gonna see who can play ball! Line up on this baseline here! Count off by ones, startin' at this end."

The boys counted off. Jomo Wade, a lithe black freshman from Harlem, was number one. Another guard, the six-foot four-inch Cranston, was second. Henry, third. Tom, fourth.

"Odd numbers are offense, even numbers defense," Phillips ordered. "Offense takes the ball downcourt, one-on-one against the defensive man, and scores if he can. Defense, play him close." Phillips tossed the ball to Jomo Wade and poised his clipboard to make notes. On the sideline at midcourt, Smith watched.

"Ball's in play! Go!" Phillips shouted.

Jomo was so graceful, so fast, as he faked, twisted and spun that Cranston, an all-conference guard the previous season, seemed inept. Jomo sped by him at midcourt, went into the air at the free-throw line and laid the ball in so softly that it made hardly a sound as it kissed the backboard and feathered down through the hoop.

A pleased Moreland Smith nodded a well-done to Jomo.

Henry, next in line, took a deep breath. Oh, wow! He rubbed his hands on the sides of his practice uniform. His hands felt clammy. Jomo Wade bounced the ball to him.

"Next!" screamed Phillips. "Let's go, Steele!"

Tom crouched low in front of Henry, arms spread wide, ham-like hands darting toward the ball, guarding closely.

Calling on all his skill, Henry advanced the ball almost to midcourt against his bigger foe; he feinted,

119

dribbled behind his back, drove right, left, right. Finally, at the centerline, he faked, threw Tom off-balance and drove past him, clearly on his way to an easy basket.

But as Henry charged past, Tom darted a long arm toward the ball, tapped it away, retrieved it, and dribbled toward his own basket for an uncontested lay-up.

Frozen at midcourt, Henry stared as Tom bounced the ball to the next man and trotted to the end of the line. No one had ever taken the ball from him like that.

He glanced at Smith a few feet away on the sideline. The coach met his shocked eye for a second, then looked away and shoved his hands deep into his pockets. Henry jogged slowly to the end of the line.

Tom patted him on the rump and whispered, "Shake it off, buddy. You'll get me next time."

"Yeah," mumbled Henry.

Head down, he saw Tom's long arms out of the corner of his eye. Down the line, he saw all the other arms, as long as Tom's or longer.

Perspiring profusely, Henry found a towel, wiped his face.

A few minutes later, on offense, he took the ball in against Jomo Wade. With a pair of fine moves, he drove past his opponent, sped toward the basket, jumped and shot.

Unbelievably, Jomo recovered and leaped from behind Henry, extended his arm and cleanly deflected the shot. Henry grabbed the loose ball and fired a ten-footer into the basket. Relieved, he again cast a covert glance at Smith. The coach was studying him through narrowed eyes.

As he and Jomo moved back to the line, Smith said, "Nice block, Wade." The coach ignored Henry.

Half an hour later, in groups of five, the boys began a tip-in drill. The drill lasted for twenty minutes, and though Henry leaped higher and more desperately than he had ever jumped in his life, he did not retrieve a single rebound. His heavy, towering teammates shoved him aside as they would a troublesome gnat.

Phillips, that worshipper of brute strength, looked to see if his boss had noticed.

Moreland Smith had. Long before Phillips.

Before ending the day's practice, Phillips put the exhausted boys through fifteen minutes of brutal calisthenics. Goaded by the shame of having been outplayed and outmuscled by his gargantuan teammates, Henry was merciless to his body, bending, stretching, straining like a man possessed. During the calisthenics, the coaches ignored him.

At last Smith nodded to Phillips, who blew his whistle and shouted, "Head for the showers!"

The coaches stood by the door that led to the locker room. As Jomo Wade went by, Phillips gave him an approving slap on the tail and said, "Way to go, there, Jomo baby!"

Henry approached the door, his face red, the veins bulging in his neck.

"Steele," Phillips snapped.

"Sir?" Henry stopped.

"Don't worry 'bout it. Tomorrow's another day."

Henry barely managed a smile as he trotted from the gym.

Moreland Smith stared after him. Sighing, the coach folded his arms. His mouth set itself in a hard line of disappointment.

"Sure, I'll accept the charges," Jerome sang out. Henry heard him call, "Eunice! It's Henry!"

"Hey, Dad."

"Son! How you doin'? From your letters, looks like you're kind of takin' over out there."

"Not exactly, Dad." Henry thought of the practice concluded just a few minutes earlier. His entire body ached.

"What? Must be a bad connection. I read your last letter to just about ever' man and critter in town. The one about gettin' your picture took with Coach Smith

121

for the newspapers. Everybody in Elroy's expectin' big things o' you, Henry. Know what I tell 'em? I tell 'em not to worry. Right, son?"

For a moment, Henry did not answer.

"Sure. Uh, Dad—is Ma there?"

"Betchaboots. Here, Eunice."

"Henry, darlin'?"

"Hi, Ma."

"Are you all right? There's nothin' wrong, is there?"

"Oh, no, Ma. I, uh—just wanted to hear your voice."

"I wanted to hear yours, too, darlin'. Henry, are you doin' your lessons? And makin' friends? I do hope you're havin' fun, and dates, and goin' to parties—"

"Now cut that out, Eunice!" Henry heard his father bark, and then Jerome was back on the line. "Henry?"

"Hi, Dad."

"Henry, your Ma's got the simples, son. Friends and parties. Bull! *Basketball*, Henry! Basketball's *your* party! That's your life. Without basketball, you're nowhere. You know that, Henry. Right?"

"Right."

"That other stuff—girls and parties and lessons—that'll take care of itself, once you're on top. You just stick with your basketball. Right?"

"Right, Dad."

Later that afternoon, he went by the athletic office to pick up his check from B.J. Rudolph.

"Happy?" she asked, smiling as he glanced at it.

"Ma'am?"

"Your check. It's for seventy dollars."

"Oh. Last week it was for fifty-six."

"Yes. Sometimes Señor Gonzales misguidedly tries to save the athletic department a dollar an hour. I caught the mistake. You get five an hour now, not four. Say, 'Thank you, Miss Rudolph.'"

"Thank you, Miss Rudolph."

"That didn't sound too happy." She rose and stood close to him. "What's wrong, Henry? Don't you like your job? Are you having troubles with your classes? How can I help you?"

"Oh, everything's fine, ma'am. No problems at all. I think I'll go study now."

He fled back to his room, sat his bone-tired body at the desk, and attacked his English textbook.

That night he had a date with Julie.

The passenger seat of the Lincoln Continental opened into a bed. Henry lay back in the deep cushions, Julie on top of him. Her lips and tongue caressed his neck, ears, hair, mouth. Her hands played with his belt buckle, undid it, and unzipped his jeans. Purring hot breaths, she pulled down his jockey shorts, played with him.

At last she put her cheek against his and whispered. "You're not much fun tonight, Henry-poo."

"Sorry," he said. "Somethin' on my mind."

She took his hand and put it inside her blouse.

"Tell me what it is. Julie will make it better," she murmured.

From an inch away, Henry looked at her face. A masterpiece. Once he had asked her why she had chosen him when she could have the pick of the campus. "Because," she had answered, "I'm the biggest beauty, and they tell me you're going to be the biggest jock. So—together—we rule this joint for the next three or four years."

Now she repeated, "Tell me what's on your mind and Julie will make it better."

"It's basketball. Among other things."

She giggled. "Well, basketball's *always* on your mind." Her fingers danced in his crotch. "But it's never made any difference *before*. Ohhh, come on, Henry," she implored him. Taking his hand from her breast, she moved it down inside her panties.

"I'll make it better," she moaned. "Mmmmm, come on, Henry. Ohhh, mmmm, Henry, come *on*."

Her tongue, in a frenzy, sought his ear, his mouth,

pushed open his lips. Groaning, she kissed his chest.

She paused and looked at him. "Henry?" she whispered.

Then she shouted. "Oh! You bastard! You're *asleep*! Asshole!"

Furious, she opened the car door and began pushing him out. In a daze, he stumbled from the car, holding his unbuttoned pants to keep them from falling.

Julie started the motor, revved it thunderously. Rage clouded her gorgeous face. "Oh!" she hissed at him.

Tires squealing, the Lincoln screamed away, leaving the exhausted Henry on the curb, three miles from his dorm.

After his last class the next morning, Henry wandered idly, books in hand, around the campus. Basketball practice would begin in a couple of hours, at two-thirty. He tried not to think about it.

He came to a grassy field that was flanked by the library, the Student Center building and a small lagoon. Students sat on the soft green turf, young men and women scattered like wild flowers in a meadow, studying, talking, napping. One group gathered around two guitarists. Music drifted gently over the field. The autumn sun warmed the air.

Aimlessly, Henry walked across the field. As if for the first time, he saw his fellow students, looked at their faces, noted their preoccupation with each other, their absorption in their books. Suddenly he felt their community, wondered what it would be like to be one of them.

He stopped in the middle of the field. The books in his hands, unnoticed a few seconds before, seemed to pulse and take on weight. He looked down at them. For the first time in almost twenty-four hours, he had a clear thought.

He would sit and read, just like all the others.

Making sure he was not observed, Henry slowly sat down, his legs crossed under him. Then he stretched out on the grass, enjoying the smell of the rich earth a foot from his nose, the feel of the living blades bending beneath his body. Opening *Moby Dick* and holding it above his head, he began to read. After only a few minutes, his hungry mind was lost in Melville's words.

That afternoon the squad held its first scrimmage of the season.

Henry, dribbling in backcourt, spotted a teammate "basket-hanging" far downcourt. His cannon-shot pass zoomed eighty feet, the length of the court. Catching the perfectly thrown pass, the teammate scored easily.

Moreland Smith stormed off the bench, raging. "God-dammit, Steele! That's not the style of game we play here! No more of that kind of pass! You hear me, boy?!"

Phillips and the rest of the squad froze. Smith rarely lost his temper, virtually never screamed at a player.

Shamed, Henry stared wordlessly at the coach.

"I don't know where your mind is," Smith shouted, "but you'd surely better get it back on basketball. What you just pulled is schoolyard stuff! You hear me?"

"Yes, sir," Henry whispered.

Loud enough for everyone to hear, Smith muttered as he walked back to the bench, "What in hades is the matter with that dumb kid?"

When play resumed, the determination in Henry's face was distorted by embarrassment and fear.

VII

Henry did not call Janet for almost two weeks after their first turbulent tutorial session. By then, he had prepared himself carefully for what he thought of as a rematch. She had attacked his intelligence; he had decided to accept the challenge, rather than submit helplessly to her academic superiority.

"This is Henry Steele, Miss Hays," he said when Janet answered the phone.

"Oh, my. Aren't we formal. You may call me Janet, Henry."

"When may I come to get tutored?"

"Well, the only time I have open is tomorrow at one. At the psych lab, room twelve, where I work. Normally, that's my lunch hour, but for you, Henry"—she laughed —"anything."

"Thanks. I'll be there. 'Bye."

"Henry?"

"Yes, ma'am."

"Don't call me ma'am. You make me feel ancient. You know, I'll bet you and I are pretty close to the same age."

Henry was curt. "Whatd' you want?"

"I just wanted to say—I'm glad you called."

He softened a bit. "Well," he said, "the first two or three weeks of basketball practice kind of kept me busy."

"I didn't think I'd ever hear from you again."

126

Putty in her hands now, he said, "Oh, no danger of that."

"Good." She laughed again, and her next words were like a slap in his face. "Because I really need that two-fifty an hour."

He hung up on her, something he had never done to anyone in his life.

Janet's lab—or, more accurately, Malcolm's lab—was an ample, open area with desks and tables for lectures, and a cluster of cell-like cubicles, each sound-proof, for experimental uses. When Henry arrived, he found Janet alone. She wore a clinician's smock and looked lovely. He returned her smile with a sober nod, sat at a large table with his books in front of him, and waited for her to pour herself a cup of coffee.

"Want some milk or something, Henry?"

"No, thanks."

She sat across from him, coffee cup in hand. "Okay, what's first on the hit parade?"

"English."

"Fan-tastic. What's your problem?"

He stared at her. "What do you think about *Moby Dick*?"

She smiled. "*Your* problem is what *I* think about *Moby Dick*?"

"Can't you ever answer a question straight?"

His eyes, she noted, had changed. They had been soft, boyish; now they were cold.

She refused to be intimidated. "Look, Steele," she snapped, "you're just trying to get a quick, pat answer out of me and save yourself a lot of work. Read the book. *Then* I'll be happy to discuss it with you."

A hint of a smile narrowed his eyes. "I read the book," he said.

"All of it?" For a moment she felt herself on the defensive. Then she attacked.

"Congratulations, Steele! You're not only the first

jock, but the first *person* I've ever known who's read all of *Moby Dick*."

"*You* never read it?"

She sneered. "Of course I read it, you ass. I was just joking. You have absolutely no sense of humor."

Suddenly, he was formidable—a young bull, his chest puffed out, his shoulders great with anger.

His words were flat, cold. "I have a *good* sense of humor. When I'm around funny people." He leaned toward her. "And I'm not takin' anymore crud off of you. Don't call me names, or I'll forget you're a female."

Her basic decency came to the fore. "I guess I had that coming, Henry," she said sincerely, "I apologize."

He went back to his first question. "What do you think about *Moby Dick*?"

"I think," she said slowly, "that it's a monumental work of art. A powerful masterpiece of great symbolism."

"What about Captain Ahab? What do you think about him?"

"I love him. He's one of my favorite characters in all of literature."

"How come?"

She laughed uncomfortably, not only at his intensity, but because she knew he was in command here. "Henry," she exclaimed, "*I'm* the tutor, remember? You tell me. Why do I love Captain Ahab?"

He quoted Captain Ahab's words. " 'What I've dared, I've willed. And what I've willed—I'll *do*!' "

"Yes!" she cried, delighted. "That's when, let's see that's when—"

Henry said, "—when Starbuck tried to talk Captain Ahab out of goin' after the great white whale."

"Yes! And Ahab was so determined! He wouldn't be dissuaded. He never gave up, no matter what. Oh, that *total* commitment! I love it when a person pursues his destiny, no matter what it is, with single-minded devotion!"

128

He stared at her. "Then *why don't you like jocks?*" he asked.

Nonplused, she stared back at him.

Satisfied now that he had made his point, Henry busied himself with the books stacked before him, then abruptly changed the subject. Opening his history text, he said, "There's a couple of things I don't understand on this page here."

Taking the book, Janet studied him. Despite herself, she liked what she saw. But she was not about to let him know it.

VIII

October was almost gone.

Dejected, Henry finished dressing. His hair still wet from showering, his body drained from an unusually rough practice session, he sat on the bench in front of his locker and stared at the floor.

Tom had watched his roommate put on his usual plaid flannel shirt, faded jeans, and worn, shapeless shoes. Now, as Henry rose to leave, Tom hurled a damp towel at him. "Wait up," he said.

"Sure." Henry leaned against a locker and shook his head. "Man, I can't believe how bad I'm playin'."

"You're not playing so bad. It's just that everyone else is playing great."

"That Jomo Wade, he's got moves I've never seen before," Henry muttered.

"You worry too much," Tom said. He decided to get Henry's mind off basketball. "You got any money?"

"Yeah. I made seventy bucks last week and the week before. Watchin' sprinklers go on and off."

"Dynamite. Let's go spend it. There's a party tonight. You're coming. Thing is—now, this is nothing personal, man—you sure could use a new set of clothes."

Henry threw the wet towel back at him. "So you don't like my clothes, huh?"

"You're a frigging mind-reader. The ones you got in your closet in the room are worse than what you're wearing now."

"Will you go shoppin' with me? I don't know much about clothes."

"I'm going to dress you like a member of the L.A. Studs, Unlimited."

They both laughed.

"I'm ready," Henry said.

"And this party will be buzzing with chicks like you never seen in Gilroy."

"Elroy."

"Gilroy, Elroy, whatever. You've never seen chicks like these." Tom strutted like a pimp and crowed. "You've got to dress mighty fine to sip their wine."

By sundown, Henry owned a silk print shirt, a skin-tight pair of pants with no back pockets and a pair of $85 boots made in Switzerland. A few hours later, they drove in Henry's car to a luxurious apartment complex overlooking the ocean, and parked in the basement parking lot.

In the elevator, Henry said, "Wow, nineteenth floor! They sure live up high."

"Man, that's low compared to how high we'll be flying in a little while." Tom sniffed. "How much cologne did you use, man?"

"It slipped," Henry answered with a shy smile.

"Well, at least I'll be able to find you when it's time to leave."

They got off the elevator, and Tom rang the bell at the entrance of an apartment. An incredibly beautiful girl opened the door. Her huge, chocolate eyes looked glassy to Henry.

"Enter," the girl said.

"Hi, honey." Tom embraced the girl; their lips met in a long soul kiss. At last Tom let her go and led Henry on into the apartment.

"Who's she?" Henry whispered.

"Don't know, man. Never saw her before in my life. Some party, huh?"

131

Only candles and indirect red lights illuminated the dark, smoky apartment. Dimly, Henry saw people, furniture. At the far end of the living room, through open doors, he saw a terrace; beyond that harbor lights.

"Hey, Tom," he said. "Smell's like someone's burnin' old leaves."

"You're kidding." Tom stared at him. "You don't know what you smell?"

"Uh-uh."

"It's leaves, all right. The kind of leaves that make you feel like you're Kareem Abdul Jabbar and Dr. J., all at the same time."

Tom led him to a group of men in the corner of the room. "This is Henry, guys," he said. "Henry, this is Jeff. He plays football. This is Max. He plays tennis. And this is Angelo. He plays with himself."

Laughter. All three of Tom's friends looked very much alike—thick jock necks, huge jock arms and shoulders. Angelo, a gargantuan linebacker, wore a cast on one arm and a neck brace. He was smoking a joint, which he offered to Henry.

"Oh, no, thank you. I don't smoke," Henry said.

Tom explained, "Henry's kind of green, if you know what I mean."

"I can dig it," inhaled Angelo.

"Hey, Henry," Tom said, "why don't you get yourself a coke, if they got one, and sit on the sofa over there. Maybe something nice'll plop down next to you."

"Sure," Henry said amiably.

He found the kitchen, poured himself a coke, and, sipping it, wandered through the crowded apartment with growing fascination. The party-goers, bizarre as Fellini extras, were too stoned or preoccupied to notice his unabashed inspection. He saw two black dudes in a corner sniffing coke and wondered what they were doing. Passing an open bathroom door, he saw a couple screwing in the tub and a girl vomiting in the toilet. Young people, beautiful in body, face and garb, danced, talked, touched, stared dreamily into nothingness.

132

A girl approached him. "Are you football?"

"No. Sorry. Basketball," Henry said.

"Too bad. I feel like a football player tonight. They're super in the kip."

"Oh."

"If I don't find one, I'll be back. . . . You stay right here."

He rejoined Tom, who was talking to his friend Jeff at the other side of the room. A moment later, B.J. Rudolph's drunken voice erupted over the murmur of the party.

"Ha, ha, ha! Get it?" she blatted. "Athletes run in my family. Get it? Athletes *RUN* in my family! Hahahahahaha!"

B.J. staggered in from the kitchen, clutching a drink, and lurched up to them. Tom and Jeff watched, grinning, as she rubbed her hip against the embarrassed Henry.

"Henry Steele! Henry, you are so adorable!" she gurgled. "You have nice legs."

"Ma'am?"

"In your uniform. Coach Smith films all your scrimmages, did you know that? And I watch them with him. The films. I watch your legs."

"Oh. Uh, well, uh, thank you, ma'am."

B.J. gulped her drink. "I need a refill. Can I get you a drink?"

"Oh, no, thank you."

"Don't move, or I'll be very mad at you. I'll be back in a sec."

B.J. staggered away.

Jeff gave Tom a heavy wink, then turned to Henry. "Hey, man," he said, "Um, would you do me and Tom a favor?"

"Sure. What?"

"Miss Rudolph is gonna screw up this party like she always does. She's already so looped she can hardly walk. Since this ain't your kind of scene, will you do us all a big favor and drive her home?"

133

"We'd sure appreciate it, man," said Tom, grinning.

"Okay," said Henry uncertainly, as Tom moved away.

"Thanks, man," Jeff said. "We really appreciate this. Oh, gimme the keys to your car and Tom'll drive it home for you."

Henry extracted the car keys from the front—and only—pocket of his new, tight trousers and handed them over. He saw Tom, at the bar, whispering into B.J.'s ear, saw her set down her glass, and turn, smiling, to look at him.

B.J. beckoned drunkenly for him to come along. Shyly, he went to her. Hooking her arm in his, she led him out of the apartment.

Henry guided B.J.'s car out of the basement garage and turned into a wide street, uncrowded at this hour of night. On the seat beside him, B.J. moved closer until her body touched his. She put her hand in Henry's hair, played with his ear. Henry, concentrating on his driving, began to perspire.

"You have beautiful hair," B.J. murmured.

"Thank you, ma'am." He was finding it difficult to breathe.

"And beautiful eyes," she whispered. "Ever since I saw you, I've wanted you."

"Ma'am?"

Suddenly she was all over him. Her hands, her body, her legs, her lips. "You're so young, Henry. Your skin is so smooth. I've fantasized about you. Now I want you."

Her hand slipped down, explored his crotch.

"Oh!" said Henry.

"Don't you want me, too? Don't you want to give me some? Please." Her voice became a sing-song, drunken moan. "Please. I want it. I need it."

She unzipped his fly.

Henry stopped for the light. The driver in the car alongside them glanced over. Henry tried to behave as

134

if nothing were happening. The light changed. Henry drove on, struggling to ignore the fact that she had opened his shirt and was licking his bare chest. Down, Down. Her tongue discovered his navel, flicked in and out of it. He tried to make conversation.

"Um, that's a very interestin' nickname you got yourself, ma'am. Why do they call you B.J., anyway?"

Her laugh was fiendish. Suddenly she had exposed what she wanted. She went down on him.

"Oh, Jesus!" said Henry hoarsely.

The car accelerated. To fifty. "Oh, oh, Jesus!" he said.

The car was up to sixty. Sixty-five. Seventy. OHHHH, God! he croaked.

Sirens wailed behind them, and he saw flashing red and blue lights.

"OH, CRUD!!!" he screamed. "COPS"

Slowing the car, Henry grabbed B.J. by the back of the neck and attempted to push her away.

"Get up!" he pleaded. "Get up, please! They're gonna throw us in jail! Goddammit! How fast was I goin'? Oh, Jesus, I must've been doin a hundred!"

He pulled over to the curb. B.J. was like an infant unable to sit up by itself. Her head wobbled from side to side and her backbone seemed made of gelatin. She flopped sideways and lay on the seat, licking her lips.

"Please, I want it. I need it. Oh, I need it," she mumbled.

"Oh, ma'am, please shut up! I gotta think!" Henry zipped up his fly and tried again to sit her up. As soon as he released her, she fell back on the seat.

The police car had pulled up behind them. Two cops got out and came up to them, one on each side of their car. Henry rolled down his window and smiled at the policeman peering down at him.

"Your driver's license, please," the officer ordered.

As Henry's hand went to his back pocket, he remembered that these pants had no back pocket! His heart began to pound.

135

Wide-eyed, he said, "One second, sir. I, uh, can't seem to find it."

"Step outside the car, please."

He got out. Speaking faster than he had ever spoken in his life, he explained, "I thought it was in my back pocket. But I don't have any back pocket. You see, I left my wallet on the desk. Officer, you're not gonna believe this, but I'm not from here, and I didn't have any nice clothes, so I went shoppin' with my friend, and we bought me these pants here, and these pants don't have any pockets, so I left my wallet on the desk with my driver's license in it. I never had pants without pockets."

"You were going seventy, kid. What's your hurry?"

From inside the car, B.J. moaned, "I need it. I need it. Oh, I need it."

Henry said, "My mother—uh, my mother is very ill. She's *sick*. And, uh, I'm takin' her home. She left the house without her medicine. She's out of her head, sir. She needs her medicine."

"Oh, I need it. Give it to me. I want it," B.J. groaned.

The cop shone his flashlight into the car. "Your mother doesn't look too good, kid," he said. "Maybe I'd better escort you to a hospital."

"Oh, sir, I think I'd better get her home."

"I don't know, kid." The policeman stared at Henry. Summoning his courage, Henry took the plunge. "Officer," he said, "I play for the Western University basketball team."

"Yeah?"

"Yes, sir." He felt faint. "And, uh, I can get you two tickets for next month's Notre Dame game."

"The Notre Dame game?"

"Yes, sir. What's your name?"

"O'Donnell. Jack O'Donnell."

"Jack O'Donnell. Right. There'll be two tickets for Mr. Jack O'Donnell at the main ticket booth at the Western gym."

"Oh, I need it," B.J. mumbled loudly.

136

The cop looked across the top of the car at his partner, who nodded.

"Okay. Get moving. But take it easy."

"Oh, yes, sir," Henry breathed. He scrambled back into the car. "Thanks a lot, Officer O'Donnell. Thanks a whole lot. Nice meetin' you."

"I'll look forward to seeing you play," O'Donnell said.

As the policemen returned to their patrol car, Henry rested his head on the steering wheel, fighting to regain his composure.

He felt B.J.'s hand on his shoulder. Forcing himself to look at her, he realized that through her drunken fog, she had sensed his horror, that she vaguely understood what had transpired. Her eyes, though having difficulty focusing, said that she understood and was sorry.

Calmer now, he started the car and pulled away from the curb.

"May I put my head on your shoulder, Henry?" B.J. said thickly. "All I want to do is just put my head on your shoulder. Okay?"

Tenderly, he said, "Sure."

She rested her cheek softly against his shoulder and closed her eyes. He glanced down at her. At rest, her face was feminine, sweet.

When I get her to her house, he thought , I'll help her get her clothes off and into bed, and then I'll leave. Her skirt, pulled high, revealed most of her legs, and he felt the heat from her body. *Maybe* I'll leave, he thought.

IX

The following Friday after practice, he went to B.J.'s office to pick up his paycheck, wondering what sort of a reception he would get.

The last time he had seen her was a week earlier, at her apartment door. She had gently kissed him good morning as he left, but the night before they had gone at each other like animals. She had taught him, babied him, ravaged him. He had explored her, learned from her, discovered pleasures he had never before imagined. But her morning kiss was cool. The fires in her eyes were banked. They had nothing more to offer each other. It was over.

Now, in her office, her smile was friendly. Her face demanded nothing of him. Relieved, he smiled back.

"Here's your check," she said.

"Thanks, Miss Rudolph."

"You're welcome. And Monday's practice has been changed to eleven in the morning, Henry. Coach Smith has to leave town for a speaking engagement Monday night."

"Oh. Thanks." Turning to leave, he remembered something. "Uh, Miss Rudolph, I have an English class at noon Monday. We're havin' a big test."

She picked up a pen. "Who's your professor?"

"Dr. Whitman."

"Everything will be taken care off."

She smiled at his innocence. "You just go to practice,

Henry, and don't worry about the test. You'll make a fine, passing mark."

"Ma'am?"

"Everything will be taken care of. Now amscray, Henry. I have work to do."

The next day, Saturday, was "Homecoming." In the afternoon, Western's football team would play its chief rival before 80,000 devout followers and a national tv audience. In the morning, before the game, Henry was invited to an alumni "Homecoming Tea" at the home of his Big Brother, Howard Brunz.

Subdued by the grandeur of Brunz' mansion on Sunset Boulevard, Henry followed meekly as his host led him from group to group of prominent alumni.

"Look around you, son," Brunz told him when the introductions were over. "*We're* the spirit and the substance of this university. Always have been. Always will be. Coaches come and go. Hired hands. But the alumni, we're family. Western forever. Someday, after you graduate, you'll be one of us, Henry. Then you'll understand what I'm telling you today." With a fatherly smile, Brunz added, "Come on in my study now, son, and let's get our business over with."

In the paneled study, Brunz closed the door and asked, "Did you bring the tickets to the A&M game, as Miss Rudolph instructed?"

"Yes, sir."

Henry took two tickets from his pocket and gave them to Brunz, who tossed them absent-mindedly into a desk drawer, then handed Henry an envelope from the stack upon his desk. As he looked into the envelope, Henry's eyes widened.

"Sir, there's, uh, two hundred dollars in here."

"One hundred dollars a ticket," Brunz said matter-of-factly. He grinned beneath his perfectly trimmed mustache and put a paternal hand on Henry's shoulder. "Just keep up the good work."

139

He led Henry toward the door. "Now let's enjoy ourselves. Have some tea and cookies and talk about the good old days. Did I ever tell you about the Fordham game in '39, when Bootsie Ramsden scored twelve points in four minutes and . . ."

On Monday morning Smith drove the squad through a grueling scrimmage. The season's opener was only three weeks away. Two freshmen, Jomo and Wheeler, had obviously made the starting team—a remarkable achievement, since Smith's smooth-working teams were normally constituted of experienced juniors and seniors.

Floyd, a senior, and Jomo were the two starting guards. Tom, Cranston and Henry made up the balance of the guard contingent on the twelve-man varsity squad. But each boy knew that Smith substituted liberally, that the number three man behind Jomo and Floyd would play a great deal. Each scrimmage was more grimly fought than the preceding one, as the boys vied for the coach's favor.

At a little past twelve, after more than an hour of vicious, virtually nonstop play, Smith nodded to Phillips and stalked from the gym. Phillips' whistle shrilled.

"Okay, you turkeys! Coach Smith's got to leave and wants me with him, so you bums get a break. Take five fast laps, and that'll be all for today."

Just before noon, as Henry scrimmaged with the team, a young man bearing absolutely no resemblance to Henry entered a large classroom. The young man carried an empty exam bluebook and several ballpoints. He went to a seat near the back of the room, watched calmly as other students took their seats. The bell rang; the room grew silent. An instructor entered and printed on the blackboard, "Departmental Mid-semester Exam, English 101." He began to scrawl the test questions.

The young man opened his bluebook, raised a ballpoint and printed at the top of the first page, "HENRY STEELE."

140

He glanced at the first test question, smiled confidently, and began to write.

Janet remained constantly in Henry's mind. He had never experienced a relationship with a woman in which he was regarded as just a human being, rather than as a celebrity. All of his prior strengths—his physical skills, his varsity status, his schoolboy basketball fame—these were demerits in Janet's eyes. To impress her required sensitivity and intellectual acumen. At first, when she had humiliated him, he had flown at his books in order to salvage his own ego, to "show her."

Now he found that the more he studied, the better they got along. Suddenly he found himself trying to please her rather than show her. And he was discovering the fascination of the learning itself. For the first time, he realized he had a brain, a good one—receptive, retentive, inquiring.

Because of Janet, Henry gradually awakened to a vast, uncharted world outside the gym.

It was a few minutes after twelve when he left the gym after practice. On impulse, he headed toward the psych lab. If Janet were free, he would ask her to have a burger and coke with him.

The classroom half of the lab was empty, and he searched the cubicles. Each had a one-way window in its door—those outside could see in, but those inside could not see out.

He saw her in the last cubicle, engrossed in an experiment, under Malcolm's supervision. They were studying the behavior of a rat. The rat, in a cage, was hooked to some sort of electrical apparatus that reacted to its behavior. Janet took notes as Malcolm spoke to her. Occasionally she or Malcolm pushed a button which seemed to agitate the rat.

Henry had never seen such absorption. Janet's eyes shone. Her entire being seemed connected to her work. Within her cubicle was another world, a universe of exciting meanings and nuances. She was learning, and loving it.

He glanced at the clock on the cubicle wall. 12:15. If he hurried, he could get to his English exam. He had studied for it; he would take it himself. He wanted to feel, suddenly, the way Janet felt, to know the sense of accomplishment that lit her face.

He sprinted from the lab and across the campus to the building in which the exam was taking place, raced up the stairs to the door of the huge classroom. He looked through the window in the door.

Too late. The young man who sat in Henry's seat looked up from his writing, recognized Henry and grinned. With an exaggerated wink, he made a circle with his index finger and thumb, indicating that everything was okay.

Walking slowly, Henry left the building and went back to the gym.

He ran for two hours on the indoor track, resting only long enough to keep from passing out. When he was completely exhausted, he went to his room at the dorm, threw himself on the bed and slept until dinner.

X

In mid-November, two weeks before the season opener, Smith ordered a game-conditions scrimmage. In addition to the regular varsity squad, the red-shirts and j.v. boys were involved. Red-shirts were players good enough to make the varsity squad, but ineligible this season for scholastic or other reasons; the junior varsity consisted of players not quite good enough to make the varsity.

After preliminary warm-ups, the coach assembled the squad. "All right—you, you, you, you, you and you," he said. "Reverse your shirts. You men are golds."

Henry was one of the boys selected. He took off his practice shirt, which was black on the outside and gold on the inside, and reversed it so that the gold showed.

"I'll coach the golds," Smith said, and barked out a starting line-up, which included Henry. "Coach Phillips will handle you black shirts," he went on. His reptilian eyes swept the squad. "I'd like to see good, tough basketball, gentlemen."

Yips of encouragement rang through the gym as the starting teams took the court. Tom, also a gold, shouted at Henry from the bench, "Go get 'em, buddy!"

Phillips' team controlled the tap and scored quickly. Henry took the inbounds pass, dribbled upcourt, drove for the basket, passed off at the last minute to an open man, who scored. A good play. Now he backpedaled on defense, guarding Jomo Wade. Jomo darted behind a pick. Henry attempted to break through the wall of flesh between him and Jomo, and got a massive shoulder in the eye from one of Jomo's protectors. Helplessly, he watched Jomo jump and score.

Henry brought the ball back upcourt. Eyes locked, he and Jomo jockeyed. Finally, Henry faked a pass, feinted left, drove right. But Jomo's long arms and incredibly fast hands won the moment. Though Henry was already a step past him, he reached in, stole the ball, and dribbled the length of the court with Henry in desperate pursuit. As Jomo went up and sank the lay-up, Henry climbed on his back and fouled him.

After Jomo made the free throw, Henry took the ball upcourt on offense. His pride stung, he signaled his teammates to clear the right side so he could go one-on-one against Jomo. On the bench, Smith rose, eyes narrowed.

Jomo did not fall for any of Henry's beautifully executed fakes. Again and again, his incredible reach and agility enabled him to block Henry's moves.

Furious, Smith barked, "Team ball, Steele! TEAM BALL! For God's sake, what is this one-on-one business! You've got four other ballplayers on your team! Time, ref, time! Tommy, get in there for Steele!"

At the bench, Henry found a towel and wiped his face. Then, with a burst of courage, he went to Smith. The coach, engrossed in the game, ignored him.

"Sir? Sir, I'm sorry for the way I played. I'll do better next time."

"Sit down, Steele."

"Yes, sir." His face burning, Henry sat and watched.

Minutes later, Smith shouted, "Time, ref." To the players, he said, "Take a break. You're starting to look sloppy. Two minutes. Then I want the starting teams back on the court. Except for Steele. Cranston, you're in for Steele."

The winded players headed for the fountain in the corner of the gym. Crestfallen, Henry joined Tom at the end of the water line. Tom looked around. Satisfied he was unobserved, he reached down inside his knee-pad and extracted a rolled-up wad of plastic. He unwrapped the wad.

"Hey, buddy," he whispered. "Take one of these. You'll play better."

Henry peered into Tom's cupped hand, in which nestled a cluster of tiny pink capsules.

"What are they?"

"Greenies."

"Greenies? They're pink."

"Never mind," Tom whispered. "Just take one. It'll make you play better."

Henry took a capsule. When he reached the water fountain, he threw it into his mouth, drank, and swallowed.

Tom patted him on the back. "You're a new man," he said.

Soon the scrimmage resumed. Henry and Tom watched from the gold bench. Soon one of the gold players wove through the defense and scored.

Henry leaped to his feet, screaming. "Thataway! Way to go! Put it to 'em!"

Tom stared at him. God, he thought, that greenie worked fast!

"Come on, Ziggy! *Hustle!*" Henry cried. He jumped up and down in a frenzy of excitement.

The golds scored again.

Henry hooted, "Whoo! Whoo! Oh, wow! Man, did you see that, Tom!" Leaping, he spread his legs in mid-air before he came down. "Get 'em!" he screeched.

"Take it easy, buddy," Tom growled, wrestling him down on the bench.

"Ain't they playin' great!" Henry yammered. "Get 'em, gang! Get 'em! Get-'em-get-'em-get-'em!"

Smith's attention was caught by Henry's uncharacteristic cheering. The coach had seen many ballplayers psych themselves into a whirlwind of excellence.

"Okay, Steele. Are you ready to play ball?" he called.

"You bet your ass," Henry shot back.

"What did you say, boy!"

"Yes, sir! Yes, *sir*, I'm ready to play ball! Sir!"

"Then get in there. Tommy, you, too."

With an Indian war yell, Henry sprang from the bench, ran onto the court and grabbed the ball from a surprised player in mid-dribble.

"Hey!" the coach shouted. "Wait for the time-out, son! Time, ref, time!" The referee blew his whistle. "Steele, come here!"

Still carrying the ball, Henry skidded to a halt in front of the coach. He jumped up and down, unable to control his energy.

"Steele, I want to see the kind of basketball you're capable of!" Smith said. "Can you show me something now?"

"Yes, sir!"

"What are you going to do out there?"

"Run fast! Jump high!"

"Good. And team play. Don't forget, team play. Now, go! You too, Tommy. Get in there!"

The referee blew his whistle and the game began again.

Henry was ridiculous. He refused to give up the ball. He dribbled in and out of bounds, ignored the referee's whistles, did fancy ballhandling exhibitions, executed a Harlem Globetrotter dribbling routine at centercourt, and concluded his performance with a blind, back-to-the-basket halfcourt shot that soared over the backboard into the mezzanine.

Henry's teammates gaped in disbelief. Smith was furious at first, thinking that Henry was mocking him, but then the experienced coach deduced the explanation. He sat back in disgust.

After almost a full minute of Henry's insane antics,

146

Tom managed to grab him in a bear hug and drag him off the floor to the bench. Smith stared at him, icily calm.

"I'm playin' a lot better, huh, Coach?" Henry giggled.

"Steele," said Smith.

"Yes, my man?" Henry giggled again.

"Go take a shower."

"Sir," wailed Henry, suddenly on the verge of tears, "I'm just gettin' warmed up!"

"TAKE A SHOWER!"

Henry's knees buckled; for a second, he blacked out. Tom and the trainer helped the slumping boy out of the gym and to the showers.

At practice the next day, Henry took a good-natured ribbing from his teammates. But their warmth gave him little comfort. Smith ignored him totally. Phillips barked at him. Worst of all, he found himself demoted in scrimmage from number three guard, behind Jomo and Floyd, to number five guard. For long stretches, as Jomo, Floyd, Tom and Cranston played, Henry sat on the sideline, watching.

It was late afternoon. Janet and Henry sat across from each other at a table in a corner of the student lounge. Henry, clad in his letter jacket, was answering his tutor's question.

". . . and France, Italy and the British Empire. And, uh, in 1917, the United States."

"Good." She smiled at him, thinking that he looked tired and worried. "Now tell me *how* World War I started."

"You mean the assassination of, uh, Francis Ferdinand at Sarajevo?"

As Janet nodded, Malcolm entered the lounge and came up to their table.

"Concert starts in a little while, Janet," he said.

"I know." She looked at her watch. "There's plenty of time."

Malcolm leaned down and kissed her possessively, as if for Henry's benefit, then went to a window and stood looking out, scowling.

"Before the assassination, Henry," Janet said, "what were the *real* causes of World War I?"

Trying not to let Malcolm's brooding presence distract him, Henry forced himself back into the lesson. "Uh, one was, uh, when Kaiser Wilhelm built a railroad in Turkey and the English got mad. Another reason was Prussian militarism."

"Very good," Janet said. "Tell me a little bit about Prussian militarism."

"Well," Henry said, "Prussian militarism was like, uh—"

"The Western University basketball team," Malcolm sneered from the window.

Henry gave him a brief stare, then looked at Janet to see if she was friend or foe.

"In a way, Henry," Janet said gently, "Malcolm's right. You see, militarism is basically authoritarian, and so are college athletics—"

"—and both are dependent," said Malcolm, joining them at the table, "on pathological and primitive attitudes. Both sanction violence. Both are anti-intellectual."

Janet said softly, "You see, Henry, regimented behavior can cause intellectual paralysis. I mean, athletes are so *busy* perfecting their fantastic skills that they don't have the time or motivation to look inside themselves. To *think*."

Calmly, Henry said, "You don't think an athlete thinks?"

"In the sense that he knows his body and controls a game, yes, he thinks. But deep inside, he's—unexplored."

148

"*Immature* is the word," Malcolm said. "What she means, my friend—"

"I'm not your friend," Henry said flatly.

"I'm not your friend either," Malcolm drawled. "What she means is: athletics offer submissive individuals a life of perpetual adolescence. What *real* man lets someone tell him what kind of haircut to get, or what time to go to bed? It's all a pile of shit. Do you really think a behind-the-back dribble has any intrinsic social value?"

"I think—"

"No, you don't! If you could think, you wouldn't be what you are, jock."

"Malcolm, stop it!" Janet's eyes, wide with anxiety, did not leave Henry's face. "That's enough, please."

"Can't he take it?" Malcolm warmed to his subject. "I thought when the going gets tough, the tough get going. Isn't that what Coach Smith makes you say before every meal? How can you guys let fascists like Moreland Smith hype you? Smith and his brethren are nothing but Nazi generals, and you jocks are nothing but Good Germans—all thinking the same way, putting on your pagan spectacles week after week, dressing up the same way in your little uniforms!"

"Will you *please* be quiet!" Janet implored.

"What about *your* uniform?" Henry said icily.

"What?" Malcolm laughed.

"Those second-hand clothes," Henry said. "And those sandals that leave your feet dirty all the time. And that ugly beard." He glared at Janet, "And her long hair and jeans and beads and bare feet. And the way you people talk. Every one of you hippies look alike, sound alike, and smell alike."

"Hippies?" Malcolm guffawed. "Oh, God. What a brilliant response."

Henry and he were both on their feet now, their hands clenched. Pale, frightened, Janet sat between them, her small fist nervously at her mouth.

Slowly, deliberately, Henry said to Malcolm, "All your big words and fancy theories, they don't mean crud to me, you hairy cow chip. You are the most self-righteous, narrow-minded, prejudiced cow's ass I ever met. You act like you know *everything* about *everybody*. Well, chicken turd, you don't know what's inside *me*. But I'm gonna fix that right now!"

Henry began to take off his jacket. Beads of sweat materialized on Malcolm's forehead, but he held his ground.

"Henry!" Janet stood trembling. On the edge of hysteria, she cried, "Henry, what are you doing!"

"He's about to employ the only problem-solving tool he has. Violence. Right, jock?" Malcolm said.

"Will you shut up!" she hissed.

Ignoring her, Malcolm continued. "Gonna settle this philosophical question with our fists, right, jock?"

"Malcolm!" Janet shrilled. "Don't say another word! Henry! Please! Please, stop!"

Henry dropped his jacket on the table and advanced on Malcolm. Janet stepped quickly between them and grabbed the front of Henry's shirt.

"Please don't!" she cried. His enraged eyes remained on Malcolm. "*Please*! He's *wrong*! Henry! Listen to me! He's wrong! Malcolm is *wrong*! Please *listen*!"

She felt him relax slightly. Gently, she put her palms on each of his cheeks and tenderly forced his head downward, until he looked into her eyes. Her body pressed against his.

"There are all kinds of violence!" she said. "Your fists. And Malcolm's big mouth. And my big mouth, too. Oh, I'm so sorry! Please forgive me, Henry! Please?"

She had stopped the fight. Henry stared down at her, felt her desperation, felt her hot, sweet breath on his face.

Janet turned to Malcolm. Wide-eyed, tears glistening on her lashes, she beseeched him. "Please—go. Please."

Malcolm shrugged to cover his relief. "Anything you say, Janet my love. I'll meet you at the box office in front of the concert hall."

"Let's skip it for tonight," she whispered. "I'll see you tomorrow."

He forced a laugh and said, "Okay. You've made your choice. I just hope you don't have to sleep with it."

Henry tensed again. Clutching him, Janet rasped, "Malcolm, will you shut up and leave! Please!"

Malcolm left the lounge.

Janet walked to the window, breathed deeply, forced herself to calm down. When the trembling left her legs, she returned to the table and sat down across from Henry. She made herself speak normally.

"Well—where were we?"

"The real causes of war." Irony shaded his words.

She smiled. He smiled back.

They began to laugh.

During calisthenics the team trainer entered the gym and looked around until he spotted Henry.

"Coach Smith wants you in his office, Steele. Pronto!"

"Oh. Okay."

He went over to the athletic department office. B.J. was not there, so he walked through the outer rooms and knocked on Smith's closed door.

"Come in."

He entered and closed the door behind him. Smith rose from his desk, smiling his most paternal smile. "Hello, Henry."

The warmth in the coach's voice was reassuring. Smith had not addressed him directly since the greenie fiasco.

"You want to see me, Coach?"

"Sit down, son." Smith motioned to a conference table in a corner of the lavish office.

"Yes, sir."

151

They sat opposite each other. When Smith spoke again, his tone was reasonable, kindly.

"Son, we have a problem with you here at Western. You're not making the adjustment from high-school to college ball."

He gave Henry no chance to respond.

"You're too small and you don't have any muscle. I've got six-foot-four-inch boys who are almost as quick as you and infinitely stronger. I'm always honest with my men, so I'll get straight to the point. Henry, I gave you every chance to make it here with us, but you haven't come through."

Smith's steady gaze did not waver from Henry's face. He said, "I want you to resign, Henry, and renounce your scholarship."

Stunned, Henry could only stammer, "You want me to—quit?"

"Yes."

"But, sir. I—I can't quit."

"You don't have any choice, son."

Henry leaned forward. "Look, sir, I'll work harder. I can build up my muscles. I'll practice all day if I have to. But I can't quit."

"Don't beg, Steele. Don't ever beg anyone for anything." Smith's voice was still calm, but there was an edge to it. "Just quit. Make it easy on yourself."

"I can't, sir, I'll practice—"

"You refuse to renounce your scholarship?" Smith snapped.

"Yes, sir." Determination hardened Henry's face. "I can't quit."

The coach stood. "That's all, Steele." He went to his desk, sat down and busied himself with some papers.

Henry rose. "But, sir—I—"

"Kindly leave my office, Steele. Get out, boy. I'm busy." Smith put on his reading glasses. He did not look up.

Henry walked slowly to the door, opened it, then turned. His voice was husky.

"I can't quit," he said.

He closed the door behind him as he left.

BOOK THREE

I

For a moment, as he left Moreland Smith's office, Henry could not make himself believe that the coach had asked him to give up his scholarship and that he had refused. Then he accepted the reality of it and went back to the gym to resume practice with the team. Fifteen minutes later, Smith entered the gym, spoke briefly to Phillips, and left.

For the balance of the practice, Henry was run ragged. Phillips put him on the defensive team; when the starters practiced defense, he was on the offensive team. The other players received occasional respites, but Henry was always in action. During set drills, Phillips made sure that he did each drill more often than anyone else. When the practice was over, there were ten extra laps for Henry after the others went to the showers.

Through it all, Phillips watched him, grinning as he speculated on just how much Henry Steele could take.

That evening, he lay on his bed, staring through the growing darkness at the ceiling. At last he took the phone on his chest and dialed Janet's number.

"Hi," Janet said.

He opened his mouth to answer, but Janet's voice went on.

"This is Janet Hays. Thanks for calling. I'm away for a couple of days. Sorry I missed you. When you hear the beep, please leave a message. Come on, now. Don't be shy."

The *beep* hurt his eardrums. Slamming the receiver down, he sat up on the edge of his bed. His eyes blazed. She's with Malcolm, he thought.

His world crumbling, he ground his teeth, refusing to weep.

Malcolm and Janet, both naked under the sheet, lay in Janet's bed. She faced away from him, her eyes wide open, and gazed at the wall.

Malcolm propped his head up on an elbow. He said at last, "That wasn't too good for you, was it?"

She rolled onto her back and looked up at him.

"I don't know what you're trying to prove all of a sudden, Malcolm," she said softly. "You practically knocked the door down. Threw me in bed and used me. For an hour. Like a stranger. Why? I don't know you these days. What are you trying to prove?"

"Whatever it was, I obviously didn't succeed. I was just trying to tell you I love you. Sorry it came out wrong."

"It's okay." She kissed him lightly on the cheek.

"Janet, my love?"

"Yes."

"You're working too hard."

"I am?"

"Your tutorial efforts, you're taking them too seriously."

"Oh? In what way?"

"One should not become too emotionally involved with one's students."

"You're a fine one to talk."

"You're not my student. You're my assistant."

"Well, if you're talking about Henry—you're wrong."

"No. My clinical, objective opinion is that you're emotionally involved with him."

"You're jealous."

"Yes. But I'm also a trained social psychologist."

158

"Malcolm, this isn't like you—us. This kind of insecurity—it's for other people. Not us."

They looked at each other.

"Go to sleep, Janet my love."

He rolled over, away from her, and closed his eyes. She turned her back to him. Wide awake, she stared at the wall.

II

The two weeks following his summons to Smith's office passed for Henry in an angry fog. Each night after dinner he went back to the phys.-ed building and worked out, using the leg- and arm-building machines until he ached. He ran laps until nausea sent burning vomit into his throat. For hours he practiced tip-ins, jump shots, lay-ups. The harder Phillips drove him during practices, the more fiercely he did what he was told.

He did it all by instinct, without volition. Since baby-hood he had known that if he worked hard and stayed sharp, he would stay on top.

On their way to classes one morning after Thanksgiving, Henry and Tom checked their mailboxes in the dorm lobby.

Opening a letter, Tom said, "This is from my main fox, back home. Boy, can she cook—and I ain't talkin' about food."

Henry examined an envelope with only his name on its face. No return address. He opened it slowly, extracted a piece of paper and began to read. Suddenly his face showed shock.

"Holy—!" he exclaimed. "Oh, no!" He stared down at the slip of paper.

Tom took the slip, read it, and shrugged. "So? Big deal, you're flunking history. I got a couple of those things last year. Go see Coach Smith. He'll fix it."

"Sure, he will," Henry muttered bitterly. He ran from the dorm and all the way to the psych lab, slowing only as he entered it. A class was in session.

From the door, he saw Malcolm at the front of the room, holding up a plastic model of a human brain for the benefit of his class. Noting Henry's wild-eyed face, Malcolm pointed toward the back of the room, where Janet was working with another group of students.

Henry saw her look toward Malcolm, who nodded, as if giving permission. Janet walked swiftly to the door and drew Henry off to a corner of the room. Her annoyance at being interrupted gave way to concern when she saw the distress in his eyes.

"I'm sorry I bothered you here, but somethin' came up." Henry searched for more words. None came.

"I'm not surprised. I got a notice this morning that my services as your tutor were no longer required." She touched his arm gently. "I didn't know whether— whether our relationship was over or not."

He missed the deeper implication of her words.

"Hell, no, it's not over! I'm flunkin' history!"

Laughing at herself, she said crisply, "Then let's get you unflunked. I don't care whether the *Athletic Department* or *you* pay me. For two-fifty an hour, I am at your service."

"Thanks, Jan."

His desperation made her want to cry. Trying to reassure him, she said, "Then cheer up, Henry. You've got no problem."

Voice rasping, he said, "They're tryin' to—" He stopped himself.

"They're trying to *what*? Tell me, Henry. What's making you feel so bad?"

"My athletic scholarship. They're tryin' to take it away from me."

"They're—? Oh, those bastards!" She looked at him strangely. "That happened to one of my students last spring. A football player. During spring practice."

"They're not gettin' mine. I just gotta pass history!"

161

"You will."

"Thanks."

"Henry—forget the two-fifty an hour. Let's whip 'em. You can pay me later."

"Oh, there's no sweat about the money. I got a job."

"But if they—"

"If they what?"

"Just don't worry about the money. Let's worry about your grades."

Not understanding the basis for her fears, he shrugged and said, "Sure." Then, as she gently guided him out the door, he whispered, "Thanks again, Jan."

"You're welcome, Henry."

Concerned, she watched him trudge down the hall.

That Friday he went to B.J.'s office for his paycheck.

"Oh, I was going to send for you, Henry. I have a message for you from Coach Smith." Avoiding his eyes, B.J. busied herself with the papers on her desk.

"Yes, ma'am."

She referred to a mimeographed sheet. "For the first road trip, you're not on the traveling squad." Softening, she added, "But that's not unusual for a freshman, Henry. Coach Smith is only taking four guards."

"Yes, ma'am," he said dully.

"*But*—Coach Smith says you're to suit up for home games."

His face showed a hint of relief, then went blank again. "Yes, ma'am. I'd like my paycheck, please."

Hating this moment, she handed him an envelope. "Here you are," she said softly.

Henry opened the envelope and read the pink slip it contained. Nodding in resignation, as if bad luck was to be expected, he understood suddenly what Janet had been trying to tell him about money. "She knew I was gonna get fired," he muttered to himself.

"I didn't know until this morning," B.J. said.

"I wasn't talkin' about you."

"Oh. Henry, I'm sorry."

162

When he looked up at her, she was surprised by the anger in his eyes.

"Thanks," he said. "But don't worry. I'll make it."

Crumpling the pink slip, he made a one-handed push shot that sent the wad of paper flying across the room. It banked off a photograph of Moreland Smith and landed neatly in a loving cup below it.

As he left the office, B.J. whispered, "Nice shot."

III

The butler said, "It's for you, sir. A Mr. Henry Steele."

"Oh," said Brunz. "Tell him that I'm—No, never mind. I'll take it." He picked up the phone on his desk. "Yes?"

"Mr. Brunz, hi. This is Henry Steele."

"Yes, Henry?"

"I was wonderin' if you need two tickets for—"

Brunz cut him off. "No, boy. I already have all the tickets I need." He hung up.

When he came into the Gamma Gamma Gamma house, the pretty coed who ran the switchboard by the reception desk recognized him at once.

Smiling, she said, "Julie?"

"Right."

She plugged in a jack, picked up the headset and held it so that it would not muss her hair.

"Julie?" she chirped into the mouthpiece. "Henry Steele. No, here. In the lobby." She listened briefly, and when she turned to Henry again her voice was cold. "She'll be right down. Wait over there by the stairs."

Henry went to a sofa and waited. In a few minutes Julie came halfway down the stairs and stopped, an impatient scowl on her lovely face. Henry rose and looked up at her.

"What do you want, Henry? I've got a date coming soon."

164

"I—I just wanted to see a friendly face."

"Well, you won't find one here. You got kicked off the team, didn't you?"

"No. No, I didn't get kicked off the team."

Disbelief made her even more petulant. "Well, I've got a date. I have to change clothes."

"Julie?"

"What?"

"You told me your father owns a factory or some-thin'. Here in L.A."

"So?"

"I need a job. You think—?"

"Henry! Are you trying to *use* me? How gauche." She sneered. "I don't see you for weeks, and then you come around and try to *use* me. Ugh." As she flounced back up the stairs, she flung a last word over her shoulder. "Tacky."

"Everything's great, Dad," Henry lied into the phone.

"Fine, fine," Jerome barked. "Too bad your Ma's in church. She'll be sorry she missed you."

"Yes, sir. Tell her hi."

"Sure. How's the coach?"

"Oh, uh, great."

"You stayin' sharp, workin' hard?"

"Really workin' hard." That much, at least, Henry thought, was no lie.

"That's my boy."

Henry looked at his desk. Spread out was sixty dollars in ones, fives and tens—his entire capital.

"Uh, Dad?"

"Yep?"

"How's business?"

"What'd you say, son?"

"How's business? I mean, down at the car lot?"

"Oh. Really lousy. Now that them cruddy Democrats are in, folks don't know what that Carter's gonna do. Everybody's holdin' on to their money. Besides, car

165

business is always bad in West Texas at this time o' year. I ain't sold a car in two weeks."

"Oh."

"Why'd you ask?"

"Uh, I'm doin' a paper on the national economy."

"Well, you put what I said in your paper. Write that in the winter the car business in West Texas stinks like a polecat."

"I'm sorry."

"Oh, don't you worry about me and your ma. We're fine. We don't need much. And Henry?"

"Sir?"

"We're the richest folks on earth, havin' a son like you."

The dealer circled one last time. The red sports car sparkled in the sun.

"How much you want for it?" the man asked.

"I don't know," Henry shrugged. "I don't know how much cars are worth. I know what it cost new, though."

"Well, it ain't new now, boy."

"It's in good shape, though."

"Yeah. I'll give you four grand for it."

"It cost eight."

"That's my best offer."

"Okay. Sold."

"You got your title?"

"Yes, sir. Here."

The dealer glanced at the title. "Okay. Let's go on into my office, Jerome."

"Oh, I'm not Jerome. My name's Henry. Jerome's my dad."

"This car's in your dad's name, boy."

"Oh. Is there something I have to do—so I can sell the car?"

"Your dad'll have to endorse this over to you. Just get him to sign it."

"Oh." Henry took the title back from the dealer.

166

"Well, I'll just have to do that," he said. "Thank you. 'Bye."

Carrying the want-ad section of a newspaper, Henry entered the hotel and approached the front desk. The lobby reflected past glories, perhaps a half-century ago. Now the place was seedy.

"May I help you?" the clerk said.

"I'm here about this job." Henry showed him the paper. "For a night clerk."

"Personnel. On the mezzanine."

"Thanks. Uh, excuse me, but is it a part-time job?"

"Midnight to six a.m."

"Well, do you know—?"

"Personnel," the clerk droned. "On the mezzanine. They'll answer your questions."

"Yes, sir."

Fortunately, the hotel was quiet during his nightly six-hour stint. Mostly, he studied. Once a guest passed out in the lobby, dead drunk, and Henry had to help him upstairs. Another night a compressor in the basement exploded, and for two hours firemen trudged through the lobby, and insurance agents asked questions. Otherwise his studies were interrupted only by huge, black waves of fatigue that burned his eyes and dizzied him. He would waken sometimes with his head on the hard desk, and discover that he had slept sitting in a chair for two hours.

From the hotel, Henry went straight to breakfast at the dorm each morning. Luckily for him, the rules in his dorm were laxly enforced; there were no assistant coaches prowling the corridors at night, making bed checks and reporting absent athletes to Coach Smith.

After breakfast he went to classes until one. From two-thirty until four-thirty was basketball practice, a grueling two hours. From four-thirty until dinner, he slept. After dinner, he studied. For an hour or so, most nights, he went to Janet's apartment for tutoring. Then, if there was time, he slept until almost midnight before going to work at the hotel.

No one except Tom, whom he had sworn to secrecy, knew about his job.

The note in his box was from Janet. "Henry, dear— Please meet me at the lab tonight instead of my apt.— Sorry, but I have work to do there before and after our hour—Jan."

He arrived twenty minutes early and saw, through the window in the lab door, that Janet was conducting an experiment with a group of students. Not wanting to interrupt, he wandered about the building, seeking an empty classroom in which to wait.

He passed a door open an inch or two, heard a voice lecturing, and began to walk away. Then, belatedly, he recognized the voice. It was Malcolm's. Curiosity sent him back to the door. He peeked around it.

It was a large classroom, shaped like an amphitheater. Students filled the rows of seats, their attention riveted on Malcolm, down below at a lectern. Henry saw an empty seat in the rear row, just a few steps from the door. Not knowing what compelled him, he entered the room and sat down.

The students, whose backs were toward him, did not see him.

Malcolm did.

He had just given his students an assignment. "By Tuesday, kindly digest pages 50 to 61. And, perhaps, we might liven up that hour with a miniscule quiz."

The class groaned. Malcolm, smiling, swept the room with his eyes and caught a glimpse of Henry in the last row. He shuffled his notes, took a deep breath, and spoke to Henry in the guise of lecturing to the class.

"Last week," he said, "we talked about Watergate."

Again, a groan from the class.

"Sorry, but since this course in social psychology necessarily deals with present-day American ethics, I

168

fear we'll refer to Watergate often. Let's review a bit. One of the things we discussed was the surprising number of Americans who *condone* Watergate. On what grounds do they condone Watergate?"

Hands went up, and he nodded at a young woman.

"For the sake of a 'higher patriotism,'" she said. "Even though Nixon's men committed burglary, forgery, perjury—all kinds of felonies—they claimed they did it for 'National Security.'"

"Yes. *Lawlessness in the pursuit of virtue.*" Malcolm wrote the phrase on the blackboard. "They felt the ends justified the means." He put the chalk down. "Give me another reason some Americans condone the Watergate crimes."

This time he called on a man, who gave his reason in song. "Because—ev'rybody's doin' it, doin' it, doin' it!"

Malcolm joined in the general laughter.

"Correct," he said. Then, louder, "Correct!" He slammed the lectern with his open hand. "*Yes!* It's okay to lie and cheat, it's okay to break the law, it's okay to violate every moral precept—as long as you're doing it for a worthy cause! Or, as long as—ev'rybody's doin' it!" He smiled coldly. "Which takes us from Watergate—to college athletics."

The class laughed again.

"Did I say something funny? I didn't mean to. Let's compare Watergate and college athletics.

"What ends do college athletics hope to achieve? Win games! Make money for the Athletic Department! Achieve excellence by spending millions of dollars on a few dozen superbly trained young athletes—in a student body of fifty thousand!

"And what means are employed to achieve these ends? We buy young men's bodies. To hell with their minds. And we call these professional athletes 'students!' What hypocrisy! The way we exploit these young men under the guise of giving them a higher education makes the entire university stink with rottenness!

169

"But what difference does all this duplicity make? As long as we win games, sell tickets, make money—it's all *okay*. It's *okay!* Because ev'rybody's doin' it!"

Malcolm looked directly at Henry now, and addressed him as if they were the only two people in the room.

"I'm the psych teacher, not a theologian. But I believe that when cheating is a person's everyday way of life, that person loses his soul. I believe that when a person blindly lives by false standards, that person is not free. That person is a slave."

He looked at his watch, began gathering his notes. "That's it," he said. "Class dismissed."

The students straggled from the classroom. When they were gone, Henry rose and stared down at Malcolm, who smiled tentatively up at him. Solemnly, but without rancor, Henry nodded. Malcolm's smile widened.

"Peace?" he said.

"Peace," Henry whispered.

Malcolm turned away and exited through the door behind the lectern.

IV

Phillips' persecution of Henry reached its zenith on a day in early December, just before the team left for its first road trip. That day, Phillips had shouted during practice, "Steele, over here. You, too, Tommy."

When they stood before him, Phillips barked, "Steele, we're putting you on a special program to build your muscles and stamina. I want you to start with a hundred push-ups and a hundred sit-ups in twenty minutes. If you don't make it in twenty, start all over again. Then, you run them stairs up yonder in the mezzanine, everyone of 'em, up and down every aisle, all the way around the arena, in five minutes. If you don't do it in five, start all over again. Tommy, you supervise."

Sullenly, Tom muttered, "Yeah."

"What'd you say?" Phillips' eyes were baleful.

"Yes, sir," Tom said.

"Then git goin'!"

Wild with rage, Henry had done the push-ups with explosive frenzy. When he began the sit-ups, Tom helped him by holding his feet for anchorage.

"Tom!" Phillips bellowed from across the gym. "Let's let Steele do it on his own, son!"

Tom stood aside while his teammate struggled.

Next day the traveling squad departed. Henry, left at home, was blissfully free for ten days from Phillips and Smith. Meanwhile, in Chicago, Western destroyed its first opponents of the season by more than thirty points. In a tournament a week later—three games in three days—no foe came closer than fifteen points to beating Western. When Smith's team returned home in mid-December, Western was number one in every poll.

The day after the team's return from the road trip, Henry reported for practice confident that having endured the push-ups, sit-ups and stairs, he could now take everything Smith and Phillips could devise.

At the beginning of the practice, Smith spoke to the assembled squad.

"We're going to have a little game of one-on-one. Pay attention, gentlemen. You will learn something." He nodded to Phillips. "Proceed."

Phillips waved toward the door of the gym, and Hit-man King, a mean-looking linebacker on the football squad, entered, wearing basketball clothes. When he reached the curious squad, King bent over and picked up a basketball from the top with one hand, as easily as if it were an orange. Only an inch or two above six feet, King's bulging muscles put his weight over two hundred and thirty pounds. He moved with the agility of a toe dancer, but his nickname, Hit-man, reflected the cruelty of his disposition.

"Steele!" Phillips snapped.

Henry came forward. Next to Hit-man King, he looked undernourished, vulnerable. The squad grew tense; the older players knew what to expect, and Henry was one of their own.

"You and King play a little bit of halfcourt for us, Steele," Phillips said. "I'll referee."

King took the ball at midcourt. Henry, on defense, played him low and tight. Backing toward the basket as he dribbled, King deliberately exposed the ball, inviting a steal. Quickly, Henry reached around for the ball. With a sickening *whask!* King's elbow smashed into his chin. The force of the blow sent Henry to the floor. King dribbled around him and scored.

Rising groggily, his hand to his bleeding mouth,

Henry said to Phillips, "I suppose you didn't see that, ref."

"Shut up, and play ball!" Phillips ordered.

On the sidelines, the entire squad had risen angrily from the bench. Tom started out on to the floor to protect his roommate, but Moreland Smith grabbed his arm. Commanding Tom and the rest of the squad with his eyes, Smith stared them into sullen compliance—they knew their futures, their lives, depended on the coach's good graces.

On offense now, Henry took the ball at midcourt. As he worked his way toward the basket, King slapped his arm repeatedly—flagrant, vicious wallops. Phillips did not blow his whistle. Disgusted, Henry pushed King's huge hand away.

Phillips' whistle shrilled. "Foul! Your ball, King."

"You gotta be kiddin'!" Henry slammed the ball down angrily, so that it bounced high in the air. King, grinning, caught it as it came down and immediately charged toward Henry like a maddened rhino. His massive body smashed the boy to the floor again, the crash reverberating through the gym. King scored, then stood under the basket and grinned wolfishly at Henry on the floor.

Henry struggled to his feet and shook his head to clear it, turning his back on King. Then, whirling, he threw a lunging right that connected perfectly with King's chin.

King went down to one knee for just a second. Then the muscled linebacker flew at Henry, an explosion of massive windmilling fists. The blows smashed into Henry's face once, twice, three times, each like a battering ram. The first punch staggered him. The next two connected as he fell.

Tom and Phillips picked him up and held him so that the hysterical boy could not try to continue the uneven fight. Half knocked out, Henry struggled nevertheless.

"You sonofabitch! You sonofabitch!" he rasped at

173

King, squirming and twisting. Only when Smith came forward and icily inspected his bleeding face did he calm down.

Blue, egg-sized welts already puffed Henry's cheeks and mouth. His chin and lips were bloody. Satisfied that he had sustained no serious injuries, however, Smith spoke to the squad.

"Gentlemen, what you've seen here is a demonstration of mental warfare, of one man psyching another man right out of a ballgame—or, in this case, into running the stairs." Coldly, the coach said to Henry, "Get going, Steele."

On shaky legs, Henry walked toward the stands. As his head cleared, his pace increased. By the time he reached the mezzanine, he was running. In a fury, he attacked the stairs, vaulting up the aisles as fast as he could, hatred contorting his battered face.

The practice over, Smith walked through the long tunnel that connected the varsity lockers with the complex in which his office was located. Preoccupied, he was halfway through the dimly lit tunnel before he realized that a figure had stepped out of the shadows at the far end and now blocked his way.

"Coach Smith!" the figure croaked.

God, he thought, it's Steele! Squinting, he saw that Henry was still clad in his work-out garb. Although he did not slacken the cadence of steady walk, Smith nevertheless felt a sudden clutch of uneasiness. Had he pushed the lad too hard? Had the boy cracked?

"Coach Smith," Henry blubbered through swollen lips, "you're never gonna get me to give up my scholarship!"

Smith stopped a foot from Henry. "Get out of the way, boy," he said calmly. "Go see the trainer. Get your face cleaned up."

Tears mixed with the clotted blood on Henry's face as he snarled, "You can ruin other guys' lives, but not

174

mine! You're never gonna get me to give up my scholarship!"

Smith lost control of himself. Grabbing the front of Henry's sweatshirt, he jerked the boy to him until their faces almost touched.

"Ruining lives?" he screamed. "What do you mean, ruining boys' lives? Why you little bastard, I *save* boys' lives! I give boys a chance here! I gave *you* a chance!"

"You're never gonna get my scholarship!" Henry hissed.

"You know what you can do with that scholarship!" Smith roared. "You can shove it up your ass! *All* the way up! *With a red-hot poker!*"

The frenzied coach realized suddenly that Henry was smiling through his swollen lips. He abruptly released the boy's shirt and stepped back, speechless. In thirty-five years of coaching, he had never lost control of himself like this.

Henry laughed. "What we've just seen," he said, "is a demonstration of one man psychin' another man right into peein' in his pants."

Smith stared at him.

Henry laughed again. "Coach, you are a great *molder of character.*"

He had gone too far.

"Why, you pernicious little hypocrite!" Smith brought his demeanor back to normal, but his words came out like frozen knives. "Before you signed your letter-of-intent to play here, you bargained with me as tough as any shyster lawyer. You ate every steak, used every airline ticket, fucked every girl we bought you. You asked for a car. We gave it to you. You asked for two scholarships. We gave them to you. Not once"—his finger jabbed Henry's shoulder to emphasize each word —"not *once* did you ever ask to have your 'character molded!' Because it was *already* molded! You knew every minute what was going on! You're disgusting, you two-faced, supercilious little phony!"

175

He pushed Henry aside and walked on through the tunnel.

Henry watched him go, the smirking triumph vanishing from his face. Smith's speech had flailed him like a whip. It's true, he thought. What the coach said is true! Jesus, it's true, every word of it!

V

He stood in the moonlight for a moment, debating whether to ring her bell or to flee. His battered face was not the reason he was afraid to look her in the eye. Moreland Smith's tongue-lashing had deflated him, made him realize how bankrupt his values were. He gritted his teeth, fought to still the trembling inside him, and rang the bell.

In a moment, she opened the door. Softly, she said, "Hi. You're late." She saw his face. "Oh, my Lord! Henry—what happened?"

The tenderness in her voice melted his resolve. He tried to answer, then clamped his mouth shut, certain that if he spoke he would break down.

She pulled him inside the apartment and closed the door. In the light, she inspected his face more carefully, and tears formed in her eyes.

Her tears triggered the frustration, the shame, the helplessness inside him. He heaved a great, dry sob.

"Oh, God," she whispered.

She urged him to the sofa and sat him down. Sitting next to him, she pulled his head to her shoulder and put both arms around him. As she rocked him gently, he began to weep.

"It's all right. It's all right," she whispered. "Everything will be all right."

The morning sun threw a shaft of gold across the room. Henry, still in his clothes and partially covered by a blanket, slept on the sofa. Janet, curled up on an easy chair, watched him sleep.

He woke, saw her near him. The sunlight made a halo of her hair.

Neither moved. For a long while they drank deeply of each other with their eyes.

Wearing jeans but no shirt, a towel around his neck, his hair still damp from showering, he sat at the dinette table and ate cereal. Janet, dressed for the street, bustled about the apartment. Between long, thoughtful looks at Henry, she rinsed dishes, drank coffee.

At last, upset, she exclaimed, "No wonder you're not prepared to take that history exam! How can anyone go too classes 'til one, practice basketball all afternoon—my Lord!—then try to study, and *then* work all night in a hotel!"

Henry shrugged. Last night she had dressed his cuts, put ice packs on his lumps. As she nursed him, he had reluctantly answered all her questions. Now she knew about Smith, about Phillips, his hotel job, all his problems.

She touched his still-swollen lips gently, as if her fingers could make the pain go away. "Henry—do you want to pass that exam?"

"I have to, Jan."

"Then—" she looked at him intently "—then move in with me."

Suddenly shy, she rose and carried some dishes from the table to the sink. His eyes followed her. For a moment, he was stunned by her proposal, and then love for her surged through him—a love he had felt, but suppressed, for three months now.

"Sure," he whispered at last.

"And when my student becomes my roommate, there's no charge for tutoring. Therefore, you now have no reason for working at that hotel. Agreed?"

Smiling bashfully, he said, "Agreed."

Janet came to kneel before him.

178

"And last but not least," she whispered, "enough with the basketball. Quit."

"Please, Jan. Don't. I can't quit."

"Darling, you're killing yourself over a silly game."

"I can't quit." His face hardened with determination.

She knew he wanted her, but that if she persisted he would walk out the door and not return.

She smiled. "All right, then. Let's whip 'em together."

Their eyes met. She kissed him—a tender lingering kiss, with only their lips touching. Their first kiss.

Suppressing her excitement, she rose and quickly collected her books and purse, a scarf. His eyes never left her.

At the door she said, "Make yourself at home. We'll study when I get back from class. There's an extra key by the stereo." She threw him a kiss. He smiled.

" 'Bye," she said, and left the apartment.

Her kiss still tingling on his lips, Henry's mouth opened in a mute gasp of joy.

Malcolm was in the psych lab, alone, absorbed in a huge book. She ran to him and flung her arms around his neck.

"Oh, you gorgeous, hairy genius! You were right, Malcolm! You were right!"

"Of course I was." Gently, Malcolm disengaged her arms from his neck. He stepped back, studying her. "I was right about what?"

"About—you know."

"You and the jock?"

She nodded. She knew he understood what she was thinking, what she wanted. Their affair was over and she was sorry he was hurt—but they were still friends and always would be.

Malcolm gave her a friendly leer.

"Felicitations," he said.

She kissed him on the cheek and bounced away to put on her clinician's smock.

179

They lay on her bed, reading. She wore only Henry's pajama top; he wore the bottoms. His arm rested on her bare leg; her fingers touched his hair. Once, still reading, he took her hand and kissed it.

Janet looked up from her book. "Henry—*why* can't you quit?"

"Lots of reasons. My dad. The folks in my home town." He grinned and mocked himself. "I can't quit mostly because of me. It's agin mah nature."

"Doesn't your dad know about you and Coach Smith?"

"Naw. It'd kill him. My folks are great, but they don't want to hear nothin' but good news."

He surprised her by sitting up and, in mime, talking on the telephone. Her delighted laughter tinkled through the apartment as he pretended to speak to his parents.

"Ma? Oh, I feel *fine*. Oh, the food's *great*. Yes, ma'am, I'm meetin' *nice* people. Made a really *good* friend, name of Nanette, or Annette, or Janet, or something like that. Yes'm, the weather's *beautiful*. I love you, too, Ma! . . . Hi, Dad! Yes, *sir*, Coach Smith's treatin' me *super!* Oh, yes, *sir*, I'm workin' *hard*, stayin' *sharp*, on *top!* Yes, *sir*, you can tell *everybody* in town I'll be a starter this year and All-American the next four years! Yes, *sir*, I know that's what they all expect me to do! You take it easy, too. Dad! 'Bye, *sir!*" Now Henry mimicked a robot's electronic voice. *"This has been a recorded announcement."*

He grinned at Janet, pleased that he had been able to make her laugh. The grin faded, and his face filled with longing. They looked at each other as only new lovers can. The room was suddenly sultry.

Taking a deep breath, Janet handed him his book. "Here. Study." Smiling, she added, "This has been a recorded announcement."

Nestling next to each other, they resumed their reading, content in the knowledge that later they would

180

make love, then hold each other through the night.

"We're number one! We're number one!" the home crowd thundered in the packed Western gym. Jomo Wade led a fast break downcourt and sent the ball twisting into the basket for a sensational lay-up. The scoreboard changed to read: WESTERN 64——VISITORS 31.

Henry sat silently on the end of the bench, wearing his warm-up jacket, while the other substitutes jumped up and down with excitement.

Looking up in the crowd, he found Janet. She waved and smiled. He managed a smile in return.

VI

It was early January.

From his desk at the front of the quiet classroom, Professor Williams' gaze raked the students as they took their exam. His eyes lingered for a moment on Henry, who was writing furiously.

By the time the bell rang, most of the students had already handed in their papers and departed. The last bluebook placed on the professor's desk was Henry's. Having watched the boy struggle on the edge of failure for four months, Williams was somewhat surprised by Henry's confidence as he put his exam atop the others, smiled, and left the room.

In a moment, Williams went to the window and looked out. He saw Henry leave the building and break into a joyous run across the campus.

Williams walked back to his desk, eyed Henry's bluebook speculatively, picked it up and began to read.

The phone rang the next day in the professor's office.

"Professor Williams?"

"Yes."

"This is Miss Rudolph. One moment for Coach Smith."

Moreland Smith's voice was crisp. "Hello, Dr. Williams. We did not receive your memo regarding Henry Steele's washing out in History 1A."

"That's because I didn't send it, Coach Smith."

"Would you kindly send it right away, please. We need it."

"I can't very well do that now."

"Why not?" Smith barked.

"Steele made a ninety-two on his exam."

The red sports car sped along the coastal highway. Henry, as happy as he had ever been, bounced in his seat in time to the music on the radio. The Pacific beaches and the ocean spread to their left, high cliffs soared to their right.

Janet's hair flew freely as the wind rushed through the open windows. Her hand rested on Henry's thigh, his right elbow kept contact with her left forearm—as if they felt incomplete unless they were touching one another.

They found a plateau that overlooked the ocean. Overhead, gulls circled. Below, the surf foamed on wet rocks that glistened in the noonday brightness. The sun warmed them, sea breezes cooled them. They drank wine until they were both a bit tipsy; they lay on their backs on a blanket, holding hands, watching birds float across the blueness above.

Henry sat up and lifted his glass to toast Janet. "Here's to you—for my ninety-two!" He sipped. "One more glass and I'll see two baskets when I work out this afternoon."

She propped herself on her elbows. "Even on Sunday? Can't you forget it for *one* day?"....

"Gotta work out *every* day." He grinned. "It's in my blood."

"Ladies and Gentlemen!" she called out like a circus barker. "Step right up and see Henry Steele, the *wondah* boy, whose plasma consists of red and white basketballs."

He put his face close to hers and whispered, "And Janet Hays is also in his blood. She is in his heart."

Half-jesting, she put her hand on his chest. "Maybe

183

it's too crowded in there. Maybe there's not enough room for all those basketballs *and* Janet Hays."

"It's not too crowded."

"I love you, Henry," she said. "I love you, and that's why it hurts. Seeing you involved in all that garbage."

"It's not garbage, Jan. It's beautiful. Maybe the way they *run* sports is garbage. But sports itself—that's beautiful." He searched for words. "When I'm runnin', and I feel like I can't take one more step—and then I *do*—I know my legs are listenin' to something inside me. When that happens, I know how those birds up there feel when they fly. You understand what I mean, Jan? Sure, the way they run sports is garbage. But *playin'* sports makes me feel good."

She kissed his hand. "Okay, no more nagging. I promise."

Henry gently pulled her down so they lay side by side, facing each other. His hands and lips began to make love to her.

"I thought you said you wanted to get back to the city and practice," she teased.

"I said I wanted to work out. And you said you wanted to help."

They laughed, kissed. Gulls cried. The sea wind whistled. Henry and Janet made love. Everything that was natural and lovely seemed to be happening there on the plateau.

VII

WESTERN 110——VISITORS 58. The scoreboard clock showed less than a minute to play, and the gym, packed at the beginning of the game, was now half empty. The contest had been a rout; the fans, now leaving the arena in droves, were more interested in beating post-game traffic than they were in the action on the court.

On the bench, Moreland Smith scanned his substitutes. His eyes rested on Henry, who looked up and saw the coach staring at him. Their eyes locked. After an instant, Smith nodded. "Go in for Jomo," he snapped.

Henry quickly doffed his warm-up jacket.

No one on the team knew that Henry had defied the coach, and he had continued to work hard in the practices, so sending him into the game did not represent a loss of face for Smith. Although he still planned to force Henry to relinquish his scholarship, the coach saw no reason why he should not use the boy in a situation such as this. The outcome of the game was not in doubt; the opposition had begun to play roughly, thus endangering Jomo.

Checking in at the scorers' table, Henry found Janet in the stands. She waved at him.

Western scored, and he ran onto the court. Oh, great! he thought, glancing up at the clock. I get in the cruddy game when there's just twenty-eight seconds left to play!

Tom inbounded the ball to him. Angrily, in defiance of Moreland Smith's coaching, he ignored his teammates and brilliantly drove the length of the court. As he flew by the basket, he banked a sensational, hotdog lay-up off the backboard and through the hoop. In a close game, before a packed house, the display of brilliance would have produced cheers. But now, as the remaining spectators shuffled toward the exits, there was no reaction. In the stands, Janet suffered quietly over the lack of response.

On the bench, Moreland Smith nodded righteously to himself. The boy's an exhibitionist, he thought; he doesn't give a tinker's dam about team play.

VIII

All fall, Chris had phoned him regularly to chat. But Henry never called him. At last, Chris vowed that he would call no more, and for two months they had not spoken to or seen each other.

And then, as Chris left the cafeteria one mid-January morning, Henry hailed him. Chris' mustache had been supplemented by a lush, full beard, and his hair hung now to his shoulders. He wore a Che' beret, a second-hand army shirt, and sandals.

"Hey, Chrissie!"

"Henry. I thought you'd died, man."

"Cut it out. I've had a few problems. Haven't been good company. You ain't missed a thing."

"Sorry, man. I should have known you were up against it. Everytime there's a game, I look at the box score. You ain't playin' much."

"That's for sure." Henry put an arm around his friend's shoulders. "Where you headed?"

"Physics."

"I'll walk you. Tell me what's happenin'. Are you doin' okay, Chrissie?"

"Oh, shit, Henry! Life here is out of sight, man! I love it!"

For ten minutes, they chatted nonstop, renewing their friendship. Henry said nothing about his basketball problems and the campaign to get him to renounce his athletic scholarship; he spoke of Janet and his love for her. Chris was delighted.

"Me, I'm spread out thin," he said. "Like, there's this chick across the hall in my roomin' house, an exchange student. Her English, it ain't so good." He leered. "But we don't do that much talkin'."

"Chrissie, you ought to be like me. How come you don't find *one* girl, and settle down?"

"Because I'm like the amoeba. It's my destiny to multiply myself."

Tom came up behind them as they neared the physics building and threw his long arms around their shoulders.

"Hey, buddies!"

"Hi," said Henry. "You think it's safe for you to be seen with me in public? Coach Smith might find out."

"Nobody's watching," Tom said.

"Oh, man! I was just kiddin'," Henry told him.

Tom grinned. "Ain't seen you around the dorm much lately, champ. Where you shacking up?"

"Coach Phillips is lettin' me stay at his house." Feeble as the joke was, Tom laughed.

"You startin' tonight, Tom?" Chris asked.

"No, but I'm the seventh man." Gleefully, Tom added, "My folks are gonna see their little Tommy play on *national television* tonight!" He caught himself. "Oops. Sorry, Henry."

"That's okay. My folks are gonna see their little Henry sit on the bench on national television tonight," Henry muttered.

"Yeah, well, hang in there, champ."

Tom left them, and they continued on toward the physics building, jabbering cheerfully to each other again.

They were friends now, Henry and Malcolm.

In Janet's apartment, Henry lay across the bed,

studying, while Malcolm and Janet worked together. He sensed something conspiratorial in their manner, and when they had finished their work, he learned that his suspicion was justified.

Janet took a deep breath. "Henry, we did some research. Malcolm and I."

"Oh?" he said.

"When you recruited, they broke every rule there is. Henry, you've got enough on Moreland Smith to put Western University and ten other schools on probation for years." Janet watched him intently.

He pursed his lips, but did not answer.

Malcolm said, "You can blow the whole mess wide open. You can help straighten out the whole rotten system."

"I could do all that?"

"I've got a better idea," Janet said. "Let's blackmail Smith! We can make him get off your back, make him put you on the starting team."

Henry glanced at Malcolm, grinning. "Blackmail is lawlessness. Right, Malcolm? No matter how virtuous the goal, we should not be lawless."

Malcolm laughed. "Right," he said.

"Where'd you learn all that, Henry?" Janet asked.

"I been gettin' myself educated."

Janet persisted. "Henry, they cheat and lie to recruit you, then stab you in the back once you're here! You can't let them get away with it! It's criminal!"

"And then they institutionalize their crimes on tv," Malcolm added.

"Hold on a minute," Henry said, addressing them both. "Tell me somethin'. Why do ten or twenty million people reschedule their day just so they can watch a good basketball game on tv? They enjoy it, that's why."

"Darling, what's wrong with you? Can't you see that—?"

"Wait, Jan," he said. "I'm not through. People don't

189

think watchin' a basketball game is watchin' a crime. People watch a fine ballplayer for the same reason they watch a fine dancer—because they're seein' the best." For a moment, he spoke almost to himself. "I'm not goin' to blow the whistle and spoil it for my teammates—just because it's not workin' out for *me*." To Malcolm, he said, "And before I can even think about straightenin' out the system, I'd better worry about gettin' myself straightened out."

He fell silent. Janet crossed the room and kissed him. "There's nothing wrong with you, Henry," she said.

He clutched his stomach. "Oh, yes, there is!"

"What is it, darling?"

"I'm about to throw up my lunch." He feigned pain, then began to laugh at the joke. "I may be sittin' on the bench, but tonight's still my first time on national tv!"

At half-time, the two network tv sports announcers stood on the court in front of a camera and delivered their commentaries.

"What incredible basketball, Mike!"

"That it was, Hal. A great half. There's some really fine talent on both squads. But Western is thin at the guard position and it's hurting them quite a bit tonight. One of their reserve guards, Cranston, is out with an injury. So after their two starters, especially the sensational Jomo Wade, and —"

"—a really sensational basketball player, Mike."

"That he is, Hal. After the starting guards, Wade and Floyd, Western has only two boys who've seen very little game time."

"And Jomo's got four fouls, Mike, and that's made him alter his usually aggressive style of play."

"That it has, Hal. Which is why Western's losing to this solid Tech team by nine points at half-time."

"Tell me Mike—during your playing days you were in many situations like this. What do you think the Western coaches are saying to their team right now?"

"You're playin' like shit! All of you! You pecker-woods are lucky you're only nine points down!" Red with anger, Phillips screamed at the Western squad. "You-all got about as much gumption in you as a week-old corpse. Hell, I'm ashamed of you!"

On the locker room benches, the boys sat with their heads lowered. Behind Phillips, Moreland Smith stood in stony silence next to a diagram-filled blackboard. Now, arms folded, he walked from the blackboard until he stood front and center, commanding the room. Under his penetrating stare, the boys lifted their heads to pay attention.

"Jomo, four fouls!" the coach began. "Goodness gracious, boy! And Wheeler! Why all that fancy dribbling? Are you showing off for your folks in Harlem? Forget we're on tv! *Pass* the ball, son! Baker! Why aren't you helping Ziggy under the boards? Drop off, son, just like I diagrammed it, and let's keep the middle closed! Tommy! Thirty-five-foot jump shots with no one under? What's the matter with you, boy!"

His voice took on an inspirational tone.

"In the second half, gentlemen, we have something to prove! Number one rankings are meaningless when they're printed on a newspaper page. What I want to know is—are we number one on the basketball court! Are we?"

"Yes!" the answer thundered. Even Henry, the most subdued person in the locker room, had responded.

"All right, then! One hundred and fifty percent from everyone! Team ball! What do you say, gentlemen! Do we wipe them out this half?"

"*Yeah!*" the boys roared.

"All right! GO GET THEM!"

As the team trotted through the ramp toward the court, Wheeler said to Jomo, "If that turkey says one more thing about my folks in Harlem, I'm gonna break his fuckin' neck."

"I hear ya," said Jomo, nodding.

The scoreboard read WESTERN 50——TECH 59 as the two starting teams took the court for the second half. From her usual seat in the stands, Janet watched Henry trudge to the far end of the Western bench and sit down. An expectant roar rose from the home crowd, an exhortation to the Western team to do what it virtually always did—win big.

Next to Henry on the bench, Tom said, "I wish he'd put me in there."

"*You* wish," Henry growled.

A referee tossed the ball in the air at centercourt. The second half began.

Tech controlled the tap, brought the ball quickly upcourt and scored for an eleven-point lead. Jomo dribbled the ball upcourt and passed to Ziggy, but the Tech center blocked Ziggy's shot and began a three-on-one fast break. Again, Tech scored. WESTERN 50—— TECH 63.

From the bench, Henry watched the players' sweaty faces; he saw hands slapping arms; heard sneakers squeaking on the hardwood floor; saw the ball zip crisply from man to man, saw it shot softly, floating toward the basket, saw it bounce crazily around the rim and drop into the hoop; he saw bumping, pushing, grabbing; he heard yelling, snarling, the refs' whistles; he saw the scoreboard changing, the clock moving; heard the crowd roar, groan, scream.

And despite himself, he watched with pride as his teammates fought back. With five minutes and forty-one seconds left in the game, the scoreboard read WESTERN 71——TECH 77.

And then Jomo Wade, driving toward the basket, was unable to avoid fouling a Tech player who had planted himself in Jomo's path. His shot went in, but the ref waved his arms, nullifying the basket, and blew his whistle, pointing at Jomo.

Head down, Jomo walked off the court. The crowd booed the referee as the public address system blared

192

into life: "FOUL ON NUMBER TWELVE OF WESTERN UNIVERSITY, JOMO WADE. THAT'S HIS FIFTH FOUL. HE'S OUT OF THE GAME."

Jomo slumped down on the bench, catching the towel tossed to him by Phillips. Smith pointed at Tom. "You're in, son," the coach said. "Don't worry about scoring. Just play tough defense."

Tom checked in, ran onto the court, and play resumed.

The crowd screamed, hissed, booed, cheered, cursed, prayed, jumped up and down, shrieked. Chris, seated next to Janet, was as rabid as the most fervent fan, but Janet sat quietly as the two fine teams traded baskets. The clock ran down. Tech scored. Western scored. Tech scored. Western scored. Tech. Western. Tech. Western.

Floyd took a pass from Tom, dribbled toward the circle, jumped high and shot. As he released the ball at the top of his leap and hung, defenseless, in mid-air, a Tech defender charged into him. Floyd spun as he fell, hitting the floor off-balance. Crunch. Floyd's ankle snapped. He writhed on the floor.

Time was called; the crowd grew silent as Western's trainer, with Smith and Phillips, ran to kneel at Floyd's side. The trainer cut the shoe, sock, and tape from Floyd's foot and waved for the team's doctor, who trotted out, took one glance at the foot and motioned for a stretcher.

The crowd applauded politely as the stretcher took Floyd away. And then, suddenly, there was only a quiet buzz in the arena. The scoreboard read, WESTERN 89——TECH 94. Time to play: thirty-five seconds.

Moreland Smith stared at his bench and at last, reluctantly, exercised the only option he had left. With his rolled-up program, the coach pointed to the only remaining guard on the Western squad.

"Team play, Steele," he growled. "Stay away from the ball. No hotdogging. You hear me, boy? Don't make it any worse than it is."

Henry's face showed no expression as he ran to the scorer's table and checked in. The public address system intoned: "IN FOR WESTERN, NUMBER TWENTY, HENRY STEELE."

Tom inbounded the ball to Henry, who dribbled swiftly upcourt uncontested, crossed the centerline, drove toward the basket and let fly a twenty-five-footer. Good! The crowd roared. WESTERN 91——TECH 94. Time left: twenty-eight seconds.

A Tech player moved the ball slowly upcourt, taking as much time as possible, confident he could run out the clock. Henry guarded him closely. As he crossed the midcourt line, the Tech man slowed even more. The seconds ticked off the clock: 00:18, 00:17, 00:16, 00:15. The entire Western bench was screaming at Henry, "Foul him! Damn it, foul him!"

For a fraction of a second, the Tech ballhandler glanced up at the clock, and in that instant Henry tapped the ball free. Tom retrieved the loose ball, spotted Henry dashing toward the basket and fired the ball at him. But Henry, catching the pass, sensed that he was too near the basket with too much momentum to chance a shot. About to hurtle out of bounds, he passed behind his back—perfectly!—to Tom! Tom jumped, shot. Two points!

The Western bench, the crowd, Janet, Chris went wild! WESTERN 93——TECH 94! Four seconds left!

Under the basket, a confused Tech player took the ball and searched for a teammate to pass to. Henry, legs and arms windmilling madly, ballhawked him, and when the Tech player finally threw the ball in, Henry's outstretched hand deflected it.

Like a panther, Henry dove for the ball, captured it inbounds. As he did, he heard screams: "Call time! Call time!" Moreland Smith, normally unflappable, was screeching from the bench, "Call time! CALL TIME!"

Henry made a "T" with his hands as he lay atop the ball, and the ref blew his whistle. Time out!

194

With the crowd going berserk, the Western bench dancing with joy, Henry rose and trotted toward the bench. WESTERN 93——TECH 94. Time left: 00:01.

Moreland Smith squatted in the center of a huddle at the Western bench and drew a diagram on the floor with a piece of chalk. He shouted in order to be heard above the din. "All right, let's calm down. We're still one point behind. Now, we don't have time to set up for a shot. Tech knows what we have to do. Tommy, we need a perfect lob pass into Ziggy. Fredericks, you set a pick so Ziggy can roll toward the basket once the play starts. You boys have done it letter-perfect a thousand times in practice. Do it one more time!"

A whistle blew.

The team took the court. The crowd noise was so loud that the gym walls trembled.

Henry and three Western teammates positioned themselves. Tom stood out of bounds at midcourt, next to the ref. The ref blew his whistle and gave him the ball.

For a split second, Tom waited—and then he lofted the ball high toward the basket.

Fredericks set the pick, but the Tech defender slid through; with the ball arching high in the air, Ziggy was trapped! Tech had successfully blocked out the area under the basket. No Western player could break through to tip-in the lob pass!

Like a ghost melting through a wall, Henry emerged from the moving mass of players. He vaulted into the air toward the basket, seemed to float there as the softly thrown ball came down. Gently, he tapped it.

The ball kissed the backboard and dropped cleanly into the basket! The buzzer sounded! The game was over! WESTERN 95——TECH 94!

The arena exploded with sound. Fans poured onto the court, surrounding Henry, and only his teammates saved him from being trampled. Wheeler and Tom picked him up and hoisted him onto their massive shoulders. Triumphantly, they carried Western's new hero off the court.

Only the dripping showers and the Chaplain's voice could be heard in the hushed locker room. The exhausted team and its coaching staff knelt and listened to the prayer.

". . . and for helping us to do Thy work with manly purpose, and for inspiring young Henry Steele, and for rewarding our endeavors with the sweet, sweet nectar of victory, in the name of Jesus Christ our Lord, we thank Thee."

Moreland Smith said, "Amen."

"Amen," they all said.

Clothed, but his head still wet from his shower, Henry faced a battery of reporters in the locker room. He seemed at ease, seemed to savor the attention being shown him.

"Henry, were you cold coming off the bench so late in the game?"

"No, not really. I felt like—like maybe I had an edge. Both teams were exhausted by the time I got in there. I was rested."

"Were you nervous?" asked another reporter.

"Didn't have time for that."

"You think you'll start from now on?"

"I don't know."

"Henry, how does it feel, playing in front of nine thousand screaming people and a national television audience of millions?"

"Different. Really different."

A crisp voice commanded, "Let me in here, gentlemen! Let me shake hands with our boy."

A beaming Howard Brunz shouldered his way through the newspapermen and grasped Henry's hand. "Good game, good game, Henry!" To the reporters, the alumni president said, "I'll bring him right back, gentlemen."

He guided Henry into a corner. "Son," he said, "the last game I saw as exciting as tonight's was back in '44 against the Bees. Jess Shirdle scored at the buzzer, just like you did, and won it for us." Lowering his voice, Brunz put a hand paternally on Henry's arm. "Bring me your tickets tomorrow, son. All of them. And, uh—this is strictly between us—in the morning a few of us alums are having a little talky-talk with Coach Smith. We want to know why a talent like yours has been moldering on the bench all this time."

"Steele! Phone call! It's your Dad from Texas!" the trainer shouted.

"Good night, Henry," Brunz said. "See you tomorrow, son. And don't forget to bring all your you-know-whats."

The trainer handed Henry a phone, and he put the receiver to his ear. "Hello?"

"Henryhenryhenry!" Jerome barked. "You see, boy! Hard work pays off! That was no *lucky* tip-in! You were *ready*! Ready! Vince Lombardi said it: 'Luck is the residual of preparation!' "

"Branch Rickey, Dad."

"What?"

"Branch Rickey said that."

"Right! And it's the truth! Hard work pays off! You're on top, son! On *top*! Whole town's excited! Proud! Here, talk to your mother."

"Henry, sweetheart. You played so well. We love you so."

"I love you too, Ma."

"Guess who's here, Henry. He watched the game with us. Reverend Wells. Say hello to him, darlin'. He wants to tell you somethin'. Here, Reverend."

"Henry, my boy! Henry, that tip-in at the buzzer tonight was the Lord's work! He knows that every youngster in West Texas looks up to you, wants to be just like

197

you and walk the same path of righteousness you've chosen for yourself. The Lord knows that if He helps you to keep winnin', you'll continue to be a shinin' example of young American manhood. You are a symbol of all we hold dear, Henry Steele . . ."

IX

The afternoon following the Tech game, Janet and Henry walked across the campus toward the library. Their arms around each other's waists, her head resting on his shoulder, they strolled silently, thinking their own private thoughts. As always, Henry wore his letter jacket.

When he had come to her apartment last night after the game, he had smiled serenely at her congratulations but had volunteered nothing about how he felt. He had only held her more tightly than usual, made love to her more fervently than usual, and then fallen into a deep, exhausted sleep. In the morning they had gone their separate ways, she to the lab, he to class.

His sudden success, his new status, left her uneasy. She was independent, mature, accomplished. Henry's background and way of life represented many things she deplored. Loving him had involved compromises which her body and emotions gladly made, but against which her intellect rebelled. Now, subconsciously, she was preparing herself for the time when she could no longer be a part of something reprehensible to her—no matter how great her love.

Someone called, "Henry! Henry!"

They stopped walking and waited for a young man, a jock, to reach them.

"You're a hard man to find, Henry," the jock said. "Coach Smith wants to see you."

Janet stared at Henry, but he avoided her eyes. "I'll be right there," he told the jock.

"Pavlov's dog," Janet said bitterly. Henry seemed not to have heard her words.

"I'll tell the coach you're on the way," the jock said as he left them. "Hey, Henry, you played one great game last night!"

"Thanks." To Janet, Henry said, "Walk me over?"

"No. I'm not a basketball groupie, Henry. I'm not waiting around the athletic department for my muscle man to come out."

Smiling, he asked, "Will you wait for me somewhere else?"

"All right. The stone tables on the student center patio?"

"I'll see you there, Jan."

He strode swiftly toward the phys.-ed complex, his hands jammed in the pockets of his letter jacket. She watched him for a moment, almost sadly, then began the short walk to the student center.

B.J. greeted him with a proud smile. "Nice going, Henry. I knew you could do it."

He nodded. "Thanks."

"I've always had faith in you."

"I know that, Miss Rudolph. Thanks."

"Coach Smith is expecting you. Go right in."

Moreland Smith, involved with papers on his desk, did not raise his head immediately when Henry entered his office. Henry stood at respectful attention until the coach glanced up.

"Oh, Steele. Sit down, Steele." Smith's tone was stern. "Steele, you disobeyed my orders last night. I told you to stay away from the ball. I told you not to hotdog. Now I read in the morning papers how brilliantly you played, how we would have lost the ballgame if it had not been for Henry Steele. Well, let me tell you something, boy." Smith's face broke suddenly into a wide smile. "I agree with the newspapers! You *were* brilliant!

200

I'm *glad* you disobeyed my orders!" The coach laughed and, in mock anger, added, "But don't you ever, ever disobey me again!"

Then he was serious. "Henry, you made things happen last night. I was wrong about you. You *can* play college ball." Smith's eyes narrowed; his tone became intense. "I'm sorry we were so rough on you, son. But this is a tough seat I sit in. My problems are many and complex. The pressures are enormous. Like a general during wartime, I have to do things as a coach I'd never do as a man. Do you follow me?"

"Yes, sir. I understand."

"When you would not resign your scholarship, I was *duty-bound* to step on you—like a bug. But while I was stepping on you, I loved you, boy! I loved your guts! You never quit. You never quit because—you're a *winner!*" With genuine admiration, the coach concluded, "No more hassles about keeping your scholarship! You have my word."

Henry leaned forward, then hesitated. Smith waited, his affable smile encouraging the boy to speak.

"Sir," Henry said softly.

"Yes?"

"The scholarship . . ."

"Yes?" Smith was still smiling.

Henry winked. "*All* the way up," he said. "With a red-hot poker."

Smith was speechless as the boy rose and left the room.

As he passed B.J. in the outer office, Henry took a Tootsie Pop from the pocket of his letter jacket, put it in her hand, and kissed her tenderly on the cheek. Then he walked from the suite, smiling.

Janet was waiting for him at a stone table on the patio of the student center. At first she did not see him, and he studied her for a moment, love turning his eyes misty. Then he grinned and climbed up on an empty stone table close by.

"Jan?"

She turned, saw him standing atop the table. She looked puzzled, but smiled.

He began to take off his letter jacket. So that she would realize the meaning of what he was doing, he did it methodically, dramatically. Each motion clean, exaggerated. Right arm out. Pause. Left arm. Pause.

He held the jacket far out from his side, letting it dangle from one hooked finger. His eyes were on her.

Then he uncrooked his finger and dropped the jacket. Just dropped it. Plop. It hit the ground. On Janet's face, sunshine sparkled—a smile of comprehension.

He leaped off the table and ran to her.

As they walked, arm in arm, across the campus toward her apartment, he told her everything. He told her what he had done about his scholarship, what he had said to Coach Smith. He told her his plan: he would work his way through school, even if it took ten years, and try to acquire the knowledge that would free his mind.

It was the first time she had ever heard him talk about the future.

They stopped for a moment by an outdoor court to watch some students play a pick-up game of basketball. Suddenly the ball came bouncing toward them. Henry caught it. He looked at it for a second, smiling. Then he executed a fancy dribble, spun the ball on his finger, Globetrotter style, and laughed as he tossed it back to the students.

It was the first time she had ever seen him smile with a basketball in his hands.

ENJOY THESE MOVIE AND TELEVISION TIE-INS

ALICE DOESN'T LIVE HERE ANYMORE by Robert Getchell (88-418, $1.50)

ALL THE PRESIDENT'S MEN by Carl Bernstein and Bob Woodward (82-523, $2.25)

BLAZING SADDLES by Tad Richards (76-536, $1.25)

CLASS OF '44 by Madeleine Shaner (84-388, $1.75)

CYBORG #1 by Martin Caidin (88-371, $1.50)

CYBORG #2: OPERATION NUKE by Martin Caidin (76-061, $1.25)

DEFIANCE by D.M. Perkins (84-010, $1.75)

THE ENFORCER by Wesley Morgan (88-366, $1.50)

GRIFFIN LOVES PHOENIX by John Hill (88-176, $1.50)

LAVERNE AND SHIRLEY #1: TEAMWORK by Con Steffanson (88-294, $1.50)

LAVERNE AND SHIRLEY #2: EASY MONEY by Con Steffanson (88-295, $1.50)

LAVERNE AND SHIRLEY #3: GOLD RUSH by Con Steffanson (88-296, $1.50)

 A Warner Communications Company

ENJOY THESE MOVIE AND TELEVISION TIE-INS

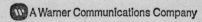

THE BEST OF BESTSELLERS
FROM WARNER BOOKS!

A STRANGER IN THE MIRROR   (89-204, $1.95)
by Sidney Sheldon

This is the story of Toby Temple, superstar and super bastard, adored by his vast TV and movie public, but isolated from real human contact by his own suspicion and distrust. It is also the story of Jill Castle, who came to Hollywood to be a star and discovered she had to buy her way with her body. When these two married, their love was so strong it was——**terrifying!**

THE SUMMER DAY IS DONE by R.T. Stevens   (89-270, $1.95)

In the tradition of **Love's Tender Fury** and **Liliane** comes **The Summer Day Is Done**, the haunting story of a forbidden love between the secret agent of the King of England and the daughter of the Imperial Czar.

THE STAR SPANGLED CONTRACT   (89-259, $1.95)
by Jim Garrison

From the first crack of the rifle, former undercover agent Colin McFerrin is flung headlong into a maze of deception and death as he tries desperately to save the President from assassins within his own government. "A chilling book . . . a knowledgeable, suspenseful thriller . . . first-rate, charged with menace. It will keep you glued to the printed page."——**John Barkham Reviews**

LORETTA LYNN: COAL MINER'S DAUGHTER   (89-252, $1.95)
by Loretta Lynn with George Vecsey

It's a Horatio Alger story with a country beat, "so open, honest and warm that it's irresistible."——**New York News**. 100,000 copies sold in hardcover!

W A Warner Communications Company

Please send me the books I have checked.

Enclose check or money order only, no cash please. Plus 50¢ per copy to cover postage and handling. N.Y. State residents add applicable sales tax.

Please allow 2 weeks for delivery.

WARNER BOOKS
P.O. Box 690
New York, N.Y. 10019

Name . . . .

Address . . . .

City . . . . State . . . . Zip . . . .

_____ Please send me your free mail order catalog